PALACE OF STONE

Palace of Stone

Chronicles of the Chosen, Book 4

SHANON L. MAYER

Shanon L. Mayer

First Printing, 2024

Cover design by JD&J Design

ISBN: 978-1-958076-21-7, 978-1-958076-22-4, 978-1-958076-25-5

Published by Shanon L. Mayer, Vancouver WA 98663

https://shanonlmayer.com

Books by Shanon L. Mayer

<u>Chronicles of the Chosen</u>
Sphere of Power
Veil of Deception
Reflections of Doubt
Palace of Stone

<u>Jen Rice novels</u>
Captives and Prisoners
Festival of Souls
Beautiful Monsters

<u>Inland Sea</u>
Star of Darkness
Eyes of Midnight

<u>Shadow Tribunal</u>
Diamond Queen

Thanks to everyone who reminded me that even when the going gets tough, the journey is still worth the effort. I never would have gotten this far if it hadn't been for all of you!

Special thanks to Connie and Jason, for encouraging me when I was about to fall into self-doubt, and to remind me that I can actually put a coherent string of text together, even when it feels like I can't.

~ 1 ~

VENGEANCE

"Master," the small hunchbacked man bowed as he entered the chamber "I come with news." The hem of his cloak scraped against the rough stone floor as he stopped to pay homage.

"What is it?" Ameil Bas-Grann, Meister and soon to be ruler of fey and human alike, glared at his minion, his eyes like chunks of hardened coal. "I'm busy." He took another drink from his bottle of beer and looked at the enormous man seated across the table from him. "You worry too much," he said. "Even if she does manage to find the last of the seals, the Cup of Jamshid has long since been destroyed."

Although Volcan was easily three times Bas-Grann's size, it was clear that the smaller man was in charge. Where Bas-Grann was relaxed, booted feet crossed and propped up on the table, Volcan seemed more on edge, drinking slowly from his wide metal cup, a worried frown creasing his brow.

"How can you be so sure?" The giant leaned forward and set the cup on the table with a loud thump, sloshing the amber liquid onto the table. "She has already proven more resourceful than either you or I expected."

Bas-Grann dismissed his concern with a wave of his beer. "So she got past your hydra, that wasn't exactly difficult." He took another swig and added, "Those things have never been the most intelligent creatures out there."

"Not only mine but yours as well," Volcan pointed out. "You had once said the smoke monster was the most powerful spell you could send against her. But you must recognize that it failed as well, not only once but twice."

"Meister," the hunchbacked servant spoke up again, having crept closer to the pair during their conversation. "I have news."

Bas-Grann slammed his bottle down onto the table, shattering the glass and sending a cascade of frothing beer onto the floor. He swung his feet off the table, which connected with his servant as he turned. "What is it?" he bellowed.

"It's the chosen, sir." As the little man picked himself up, he straightened his rough brown cloak, where it had fallen open to reveal rough green skin with raised brown warts covering his arms.

Both Bas-Grann and Volcan turned to face him, their attention riveted. Volcan was the first to speak. "Has the Djieien succeeded, then?" A small smile played at the edges of his mouth in anticipation.

The servant shook his head. "It has been destroyed."

"Impossible," Volcan roared as he shot to his feet, no trace of the threatened smile remaining. "The Djieien is an Ancient; there is no way to destroy it."

The tiny man quailed beneath the combined wrath of the two men. "She found its heart."

"What nonsense is this?" Volcan demanded but Bas-Grann raised a calm hand to stop him.

"As we both know," he explained, his voice chillingly low, "even the Ancients such as yourself can be killed. It would appear that this chosen is a bit more capable than either of us expected."

"More than you expected, perhaps," Volcan turned his ire on the tattooed man. "But I was just telling you that we should come up with another plan to stop her."

As the servant scurried out of the room, thankful that his skin had been left intact, Bas-Grann smirked at the giant smith. "And just what do you think I've been doing while you've been busy playing with your new little pet?"

"As far as I can tell, you've been doing nothing," Volcan retorted. "That insolent little human has been running through every obstacle we've put before her and all you have done is sit back and watch it happen."

Bas-Grann's eyes hardened at the insult. "Do not test me." His voice was icy, but he stood up and stalked across the room toward another door. "You sent the Djieien after her, which kept her occupied and for that I will let your insult slide." He looked over his shoulder to make sure the giant was following. "But do not expect such generosity in the future.

"While the chosen was running from your spider, as I was saying, I was gathering my forces. Much of feykind is behind me at this point and I have infiltrated every Council of Fey in existence. Every move she or any other chosen makes from this point on, I will know about."

He stepped into a wide hallway, which was lit by torches set into sconces against the walls at five-foot intervals. "But even more importantly, I have found a much better weapon to use against her." He stopped at a doorway and looked back at Volcan. "If you wish to see, I will show you."

Volcan looked at the closed door eagerly but with a small amount of concern. "What could you have possibly found that would be more effective against her than the Djieien?" he asked after a moment's pause.

With a grin of delight, Bas-Grann pushed the door open. The room beyond was small, barely wider than the hall that they were standing in, leaving no room for the giant man to enter. The room contained only a tall, slender cloaked figure and a marble statue of a woman wearing a strange helmet. The Meister stepped inside and looked at the cloaked person. "Is she ready?"

"She is," a voice responded from beneath the cloak's hood. A golden hand reached out from between the folds of the cloak to run a single finger down the statue's arm. "I cannot waken her."

"Of course you can't," Bas-Grann chuckled. "This magic is far more powerful than what you possess." He turned to face the statue and placed a hand on top of its head.

As he recited an incantation, the tattoos along his arms began to glow and his eyes changed from coal-black to red-hot light. Slowly, as he chanted, chunks of white marble began to slough off of the statue and fall to the floor, shattering into dust as they connected with the black stone floor.

"Awaken," he commanded at the end of his casting. "There is much work to be done."

The last of the marble fell to the floor, revealing a beautiful woman. She had pale white skin, almost as light as the stone that had covered her, and deep, emerald-green eyes. Tiny, shimmering green scales surrounded both of her eyes, and as she turned them to survey the room, they landed on Bas-Grann. "You have freed me," she said, her voice soft and sweet. "I have been waiting for a thousand years for this." A slow, sinister smile spread across her face as she looked between the dark man, the cloaked figure and the giant beyond the doorway.

"Oh," she chuckled. "This is going to be fun!"

LONELY STATUE

Morgan Lafayette looked out the window from her second-story classroom, watching as a pair of butterflies danced back and forth on the other side of the glass. She knew that she should be reading the chapter on the people of ancient Greece, but she just wasn't interested in the topic. She was far more interested in watching the peri as they danced to music that only they could hear.

She was the only one who realized the butterflies were actually tiny fairy creatures called peri. To the rest of the human population, they appeared to be brilliant orange butterflies, beautiful and frivolous but nothing particularly special. This particular pair had appeared around a week beforehand, much to Morgan's delight.

For the last seven months, Morgan had been living the normal life of an average human, attending classes at her dreary high school during the day and pretending to do homework at night. For most people, a normal daily existence such as hers had been to be expected but Morgan was growing impatient. She was a chosen, a human emissary selected due to her bloodline to work with the fey, defending them against all sorts of attacks. She had travelled into an active volcano, been kidnapped by a tribe of feral pygmies, visited temples inhabited by merfolk far below the surface of the ocean, even defeated an unkillable creature. In comparison with all of that, completing an assignment on a book she had no intention of reading just wasn't as exciting.

Thankfully, her mother had relented and allowed Morgan to take an art class. She had been begging for years and drawing in secret but her mother had refused. Susan Lafayette believed drawing to be a waste of Morgan's time but had recently had a change of heart. She believed that Morgan's withdrawal from everyone shortly after the family moved to Denver Heights was due to the move and missing all of her friends, which was partially true. The real truth was that Morgan hadn't even been home the majority of the time, she had been out working with the fey.

Until the pair of peri had appeared, her best friend, a haltija named Tilson, had been the only fey that she regularly saw. A couple of the others had been to see her, primarily just to visit and ensure that she was still alright, but none of them stayed for long. The massive black panther named Tekli had been by to check on her just the other day but that had been the first time she had seen any of the big cats in months.

Even Askel, the gryphon with whom she had formed a bond long ago, had been strangely absent for about two months. He had come by every week or so but had suddenly disappeared. As many times as she had asked, a reason for his absence hadn't yet been given and she missed him dearly.

On her way home from school that afternoon, she spotted a familiar figure. The haltija, a regular companion of hers while working in service to the fey, was lounging on the hood of a car, busily working his way through a small pile of grapes.

"Any news?" she asked when she got closer. The first handful of times she had encountered her friend, she had immediately become excited in the belief that he had been sent to retrieve her. When his appearances had proven to be nothing more than casual visits, she had been disappointed. Since those first handful of times, she no longer assumed anything.

"Nope," he said as he stuffed another grape into his mouth. "Just keeping our eyes open in case something happens."

She let out a resigned sigh. It was the same answer he always gave. "I barely see anyone anymore," she grumbled. "The least you guys could do is to stop by and visit more often."

"Corran says we need to give you your space so you can keep up with stuff happening in your human world," Tilson said as he finished chewing the last grape and scampered up to perch in his usual spot on her shoulder. When she had first discovered the existence of the fey, Morgan had been concerned about having Tilson or any of the others near her out in public, worried as to how the other humans would react at the sight of him. Her concerns had been for nothing because Tilson, as with all of the rest of the fey, was covered in a magical glamour that kept him from being visible to humans unless he decided otherwise.

"I know. But everyone's been gone for so long now, I was starting to get worried. Particularly about Askel."

"Why Askel?" the haltija asked. "What's wrong with him?"

"I have no idea," Morgan answered. "He was coming by every now and then until a couple months ago, but I haven't heard anything from him since then." While she was certain that the gryphon could take care of himself, she was still worried about her friend. "Do you know what he's been up to?"

"Nope. Last I saw him was about the same

amount of time ago. Probably off minding his own business somewhere."

"Speaking of the last time I saw people; do you have any idea why I haven't been called at all? I know," she added before he could respond, "Corran wants me to settle in with my own people. But it's been months!"

"I really don't know," he said. "But I just wanted to check in on you. I really do need to get going." He leaped from her shoulder, landing in a soft patch of grass. "Don't worry," he called behind him as he scampered away. "They'll call for you as soon as they need you."

"Yeah, right," she grumbled, more to herself than to anyone else. She hadn't really expected Tilson to have any answers for her, she just wished she knew why it had been so long since she had been needed.

As she walked past a row of storefronts, she thought she saw a pair of clear blue eyes watching her from the reflection on the windows. Her heart skipped a beat, as it did every time she thought she had spotted the Mirror Man, a strange half-human, half-fey Ancient she had met almost a year previously. Although their meeting had been short, he had left a distinct impression on her. The first few times she had encountered him, she had barely been able to control herself. That reaction had been due to an effect from his magic, she had learned. Even after she was no longer susceptible to his aura effect, he was still on her mind much more often than she would have expected. When she turned to look, hoping to see his curious face looking back at her, there was nothing to see. The glass was empty save for her own reflection.

"Probably just my imagination," she reasoned to herself. It wasn't the first time she had thought she'd seen him watching over her. Every time, he disappeared as soon as she spotted him, making her wonder whether she was actually seeing him or whether it was just wishful thinking.

It wasn't even as though she hadn't seen any of the fey at all. The fey she had seen, rather than being the ones with whom she had forged a friendship, seemed intent on causing as much destruction and havoc in the human world as possible. She had been on her guard constantly in order to keep them from doing too much damage. "Even if they aren't calling on me to help, I'm still gonna do my part to help them."

A strange creature had recently moved into the park a few blocks away from the school. There, he had been slowly moving through the playground and destroying most of the equipment housed there. So far, she hadn't come up with a good way to stop his damage but that didn't mean she wasn't still trying. She stepped into the park, a normal shortcut on her way home, and headed directly toward the beast. Since most of the fey she could ask about it had been absent, Morgan hadn't been able to uncover what the creature was, let alone get any advice on stopping it.

It stood almost six feet tall, well taller than Morgan was, with dark burgundy skin and a bright green eye in the center of its forehead. Pointed ears rose above the top of its misshapen, lumpy head. Morgan was careful not to get too close to the beast, as it smelled like vomit that had been sitting out in the summer heat. At that particular moment, it was sitting on top of the swing set, kicking absently at the bars holding it aloft. Rather than dealing with the creature at that moment, Morgan continued walking, barely giving the hideous creature a second glance.

She wasn't the only one who had noticed the strange levels of destruction in the park, as well as elsewhere in town. Her mother had commented on it that very morning, having just finished watching the news. Even a couple of the students had been discussing the vandalism over lunch period. Cars and homes had been damaged, possibly by the creature in the park but also possibly by other fey beasts as well. Morgan herself had seen a group of small creatures as they had crept up on her father's car one night. The fact that she could see them was likely the only reason they had left her family alone.

The worst places of all areas in town were the intersections. Nobody trusted them anymore. Even if the traffic light was green, which usually meant it was safe to pass through, that didn't automatically mean that the oncoming traffic didn't have a green light as well. It had only taken a couple of people being hospitalized due to collisions before drivers and pedestrians alike became distrustful of street lights.

As she passed the post office, she spotted something she hadn't noticed before. A statue, carved from stone the same color as the street next to it, stood alongside the sidewalk. The statue was in the form of a little boy, perhaps ten years in age, wearing school clothes with a backpack slung across his shoulders. "When did this get put here?" she wondered as she walked past it.

As she looked more closely, she appreciated how lifelike the statue was. It could easily have been a real person, replicated to exacting measures in stone. She had seen something similar in a museum once, statues created hundreds of years ago that looked almost as lifelike as the boy next to her.

"No," she whispered to herself as recognition dawned. "It can't be. How did he get turned into stone?" The boy looked so lifelike, in fact, that he appeared exactly the same as the posters that had popped up all over town the last couple days, notices posted by a pair of worried parents searching for their missing son. "How did nobody see you here?"

She looked around the area, searching for someone to wave over for help, but realized it would be futile. "Can they even see you? Is that why you're still here? Who would believe me?" she wondered. "People don't just turn into stone like that." Even worse, should someone be able to actually see the statue and for some reason believe that it was the missing child, how could they turn him back to flesh again?

She continued to search the area, no longer seeking aid from the human population but changing her focus to find one of the fey. Although they had been leaving her alone, keeping their distance for the last few months, they were never far away, always watchful of the goings-on in the human world. Spotting a peri, she waved him over, recognizing him as the same orange-winged fey that had fluttered by her classroom window only an hour before.

"You need to contact Corran and the others on Zea Island," she explained when the peri got closer. "They need to know what's going on."

"And what would that be?" the peri asked

as he alighted on a fencepost. "Or are you still upset about the cyclops in the park?"

"The what?" Morgan was confused for a moment before shaking it off. "No, well yes but that's not what I'm talking about right now. They need to know about him." She pointed at the statue with emphasis.

"It's a statue," the peri eyed her with confusion. "You humans have those things everywhere."

"Not like this," she explained. "This was a person just a few days ago. People don't just turn into stone like that. You guys must have some idea of how to fix him." Magic, the life force of all feykind, was the only way she could imagine of turning a human being into a stone statue. If magic had caused the change, then it stood to reason that there would be magic to undo the change.

"I'll let them know," the peri said, looking between her and the statue doubtfully. "Just looks like a statue to me, though."

"Just tell them about it," she responded in exasperation. "I'm going to see what else I can find."

The peri took off and quickly disappeared from view. Once he was gone, Morgan hitched her backpack higher on her shoulder, wishing it was the satchel she used while working with the fey. Her satchel held an assortment of items, none of which did she think would help her at that moment but just about anything would be more useful than a textbook on basic algebra and a half-chewed pencil.

She wished, not for the first time, that she had a way to contact Stormshock but the enormous green dragon was still in hiding and she didn't dare to even mention his name in public. Not because of the humans, of course, but because of the fey. He had only barely managed to escape the failed attempt on his life and even Morgan had believed him to be dead until recently. She wasn't willing to risk anything that could cause another attempt on her friend, one of the few dragons who had survived the mayhem.

As she made her way back home, she kept an eye open for any other strange statues but spotted none. Upstairs in her bedroom, she dropped her backpack onto the floor next to her bed where she normally stored it when she was home and headed for her closet. The closet was filled with an assortment of laundry that had been neither folded and placed into her dresser nor hung on the empty hangers above but she ignored the layers of jeans, socks and sweaters, focused instead on the brown strap that peeked out from beneath and behind the pile. With a tug, the satchel slipped free of its hiding place.

With her other hand, she withdrew a wooden pole that was only slightly shorter than Morgan herself was. It had worn leather straps wound and tied around one end with a small yellow stone dangling from one of the cords. The pole was more than just a decorated stick, the Staff of Survival had been gifted to her by a druid she had met almost a year previously. It held a number of enchantments that had saved her life on more than one occasion. She set the satchel onto her bed, pulled a green cloak from its thumbtack and stuffed it inside, and then leaned the staff next to it before heading downstairs to resupply her pack.

A handful of granola bars, a fresh set of batteries for her flashlight, and a small bottle of orange juice joined the jumble of items in the satchel. Once everything was secured inside and her favorite hooded sweatshirt was looped over the top of the pack, she walked over to the window to wait. It was still too warm outside to wear the sweater but she had learned through experience that the weather where the fey sent her was rarely the same as the weather at home.

"Good, you're ready." Tilson crawled in through the window and perched on the sill. "I was hoping you wouldn't take too long to get packed this time."

"Yep," she responded. She picked up her satchel and staff and followed the haltija out the window. She had hoped to see Askel waiting outside to take her to the island, but the familiar brown and white gryphon was nowhere to be found. Instead, she found a different gryphon, this one with black fur and dark brown feathers. "Glau," she called over to him. "Nice to see you again."

"And you as well," Glau said. None of the gryphons Morgan had met communicated in human speech but the tree-shaped amulet around her neck, gifted to her by the same druid as the staff, allowed her to communicate with almost any of the fey with whom she came into contact, Glau included. She hadn't needed to remember to put on the amulet, as it had long since become a staple around her neck, even when she was stuck in class all day.

She took a moment to smooth the soft feathers on Glau's neck before climbing onto his back. She loved riding on the gryphons, the feeling of flying with them was one of her favorite things about working with the fey. As she felt the world drop away beneath a powerful beat of Glau's wings, she smiled for what felt like the first time in months.

The trip to Zea Island was swift, as the meeting place of the fey was reasonably close to her own home. Most of the human population had no idea that there was an island in the center of the river, as it was hidden by the same magic as that which kept the fey hidden from the human world. Because of how long Morgan had been working as a chosen, she had grown accustomed to the magical barrier between worlds known as the veil, so everything on both sides of the glamour was visible to her. She watched with interest as they circled the island before coming in to land in the clearing at the center.

"Greetings, Morgan." A tall man with shimmering golden skin and silvery-white hair spread his arms wide to bow as she slipped to the ground. "I trust you have been well."

"I have," she included the elvor in her smile. "But I was starting to wonder if I was being retired as chosen, considering how long it's been since I heard from any of you."

Corran's return smile didn't quite reach his eyes. "No, you were not replaced but a great deal has been happening in your absence and we felt it was safer for you to stay in your world until we knew more of the troubles we are facing."

"Couldn't possibly be any worse than the Djieien," Morgan muttered as the elvor turned to lead her to the edge of the clearing. Although she was happy that she hadn't been replaced as chosen, she was frustrated at the fey's insistence of keeping her from knowing what was going on with her friends. Even the summons to Zea Island was less of a request for her presence than a demand. Corran spoke for the Council of

Fey, a secretive group that controlled both the activities of the fey and those of Morgan while she was in service to them. Requests from the council, voiced as invitations as they so often were, were never an optional thing. When Corran called for her, she was brought to him, period. For her to have requested the meeting as she had done this time was the exception.

"If there was so much going on," she called after him, "why did you guys leave me out of it for so long? You guys brought me in plenty of times when you didn't know what was going on before, so what makes this time so different?" What she really wanted to know but didn't dare put to voice was why she was being constantly ignored. If her work as their chosen was so important, which all of the fey seemed to believe, then why had she been left alone for so long? Was she just not needed?

"The statue you spotted in your human town," Corran ignored everything she had just asked, as usual, "wasn't the first of these attacks. The council has heard of others turned to stone just as your human boy was. We don't know the cause of these attacks or the reason behind them, but it is not just occurring in your world." He turned to face her. "Many of our kind have been turned to stone as well. Until your report, we had been unaware that both humans and fey were being targeted this time. We had hoped to keep you safe in your world until we uncovered either the source of the stoning or a treatment to restore them back to life but it seems that time has run out."

"You don't have a way to fix them?" Morgan asked in surprise. She hadn't considered that the fey would be at as much of a loss in the situation as she herself was. "What do we do?"

"First, we need to know everything you know about the human boy. I don't need to know who he was or what his interests were, I just need to know how long ago he was turned to stone."

Morgan explained how long the child had been missing before she discovered his statue and answered all of Corran's questions as much as she could. She also explained about the other strange creatures that had been making a mess in the human world while she had been there, including the creature in the park that the peri had called a cyclops. To her dismay, the elvor seemed less interested in the chaos-wreaking fey in the human world, focused intently on everything she knew about the statue.

"I think that will be enough for us to get started on our end," Corran said when she was done. "For your part, we need to know more. While the information you have given us is more than what we had, it is still not quite enough for us to be certain of much. We ask of you to go back into your world and see if there are any more statues, either human or fey, that had not yet been uncovered. Any you find, we will retrieve and bring here so that once a treatment is found, they can be restored and returned to their lives. Askel will assist you in this. His eyesight may prove useful."

As though waiting for his name to be spoken, Askel dropped from the sky and jogged over to join them. Her grin widened at the sight of her dear friend. Much as she loved Glau, she much preferred working with Askel.

"The statue in Denver Heights has the council concerned," he explained as they flew back to town. "As have all of the other incidents. Although I doubt Corran mentioned anything, the council has been monitoring the situation in the human world closely."

"Do you know why I've been kept in the dark for so long?"

"There are things which even I do not know," he chuckled. "Are you certain you are ready for this?"

"I'm ready," she assured him. "I've been ready for seven months. Let's do this."

~ 3 ~

STONE SILENT

Their first stop was to the post office, where the statue of the boy remained undisturbed. It waited in the same shady corner of the lawn, just off of the sidewalk, as it had been when Morgan had first discovered it. The grass around the statue appeared to have been recently mowed and Morgan looked in surprise at the swirled pattern in the grass.

"It looks like they ran the lawnmower through here today," she pointed out, "and they just swerved around the statue here as though it was supposed to be here." Despite the amount of time she had spent as a chosen and the many ways in which the humans avoided contact with anything from the world of the fey, it never ceased to amaze her exactly how oblivious humans were to their interactions with another world. Shaking her head in a combination of amusement and befuddlement, she stepped closer for a better look.

The boy appeared to have stopped mid-stride, his face turned at a slightly upward angle and his eyes wide open, as though someone had surprised him or caught his attention in some way. A stone stick, likely a random interest that the boy had picked up and carried with him, was grasped loosely in one hand, angled toward the ground.

"He doesn't look frightened," Tilson pointed out as he hopped up to perch on the boy's head.

"Get off of him," Morgan chided him. "No, he doesn't. I'd say he looks more curious than scared."

"What does that mean?" Askel asked.

"Not sure," Morgan admitted. "Could mean any number of different things. I think we can pretty easily rule out any of the human population causing this, first of all. I may not know a whole lot but if there is a way to turn people into stone, it'd probably be known about already." There was one means by which it could happen naturally but it seemed like a far-fetched idea, at best. "The only thing I can think of from the human world that could cause something like this would be petrification but that takes a lot of years to happen so I think we can rule that out here.

"Besides," she added, "Corran said fey were being attacked too. That means that unless it's a chosen like me causing it, there's probably some sort of fey at the source."

"Agreed," Askel said. "I believe the council came to the same conclusion."

She nodded. "I would guess that most people would be pretty surprised if one of you guys popped up in front of them and became visible. In this case, though, I'm not sure that's gonna help much."

"Why not?" Sulking over being chastised for perching on the statue, Tilson sat on Askel's back, arms crossed over his tiny chest.

"Because kids are more open to strange things," she reminded him. "That's why you guys always choose kids to be your chosen, remember?"

Both Tilson and Askel nodded their agreement to her observation, so she continued. "Assuming that there's a fey in play here, I think we can narrow it down a little bit."

"How so?"

"Well, look at him." She stepped aside and gestured to the boy's face. "He's not scared. Sure, he's a little surprised and probably pretty curious but he doesn't look like he just saw something scary. That would rule out a lot of the fey I've been dealing with. Gigantic spiders, stinky ogres, had he seen something like that, he'd probably be a bit more scared."

"There's the size, too," Tilson pointed out as he jumped down to Morgan's shoulder. "He's not looking up. Believe me," he puffed out his chest and waved his tail indignantly, "he's either looking at something that's really big and not very close or something that's not too big but a lot closer."

"Or something that was flying," Morgan agreed. "I suppose a magic wand or something like that could have caused this also," she mused. She had used a magic wand on more than one occasion herself, in fact one was currently tucked into her satchel. "They can have a bit of range on them and most people aren't scared when someone points a stick at them."

"Maybe he was playing wand fight," Tilson pointed out. "Look, he's carrying a wand too."

Morgan examined the stick in the boy's hand more closely. What she had first thought was just a random object could have been more of a clue than she had first thought. "Could be," she admitted finally. "But I think we need more than just one example to really know what we're dealing with here."

Tilson looked at her, aghast. "You want to just stand around waiting for someone else to get turned into stone?"

"Of course not. But he's not the only one like this. Remember? Corran said that others had been turned to stone too, not just humans. If we go and look at some of the other statues, we might get a better idea of what we're looking for."

With nothing more to discover from the boy's statue, Morgan, Askel, and Tilson went in search of more statues. "It's still surprising to me," Morgan mused as they walked, "that nobody even gave him a second glance. It's like they just didn't even notice he was there."

"That's the glamour," Askel reminded her.

"I know," she admitted, "but what I'm saying is that if people didn't even recognize one of their own, they aren't very likely to pay any more attention to a statue of an imaginary creature like one of you."

It didn't take long for the group to discover more statues. The first was discovered by Tilson, who pointed out the peri perched on the branches of a tree. The next was a creature Morgan hadn't encountered before, a short man with curved horns atop his head and the legs and feet of a goat. She had seen goat-men before but those had four legs in the lower half of their bodies and were called apotharni. This one had two legs and was much smaller than the apotharni she knew.

"Satyr," Arien supplied to her inquiring glance. "Yes, he is one of ours."

"Wonder what he was doing here," Tilson added. "Satyrs generally don't like humans all that much, they tend to stay in the forests and such."

"I think I heard of them once before," Morgan said, "but I hadn't come across any yet." She slowly walked around the statue, wondering what it was doing in town. Sure there were trees all around but not even remotely plentiful enough to be called a forest, even by the wildest stretching of the truth.

"Do you think it might be some sort of a trap?" She knew that there were traitors in the Council, at least one but likely more than that. So far, neither she nor any of the other council members had uncovered who the traitor was but that didn't mean a whole lot, in her opinion.

She had her own suspicions about the traitor's identity but she wasn't certain enough of anything to put name to any of them yet. The highest on her list, much as she didn't want to admit it, was Corran. The elvor had lied to her on at least one occasion in the past but despite that she had a hard time viewing him as a traitor or believing that he could be trying to harm her.

Not just her, she realized. In all of the

previous times she had been called to assist the fey, it had been the fey alone who had been targeted. This time, however, the danger threatened the entire human population as well.

"We should go let them know what we found out," Tilson suggested. "Maybe the council has found something while we're out here finding a whole lot of nothing."

"I'm not quite sure I'm ready to go back yet," Morgan said slowly, trying to come up with some other avenue to investigate. As she scanned the area, she realized that with Askel finally at her side once more, there was another place to look, another point of contact that they could make. Unable to fly under her own power, not even knowing precisely where it was she needed to go, she hadn't been able to reach out to this particular person until now. With the gryphon's assistance, however, she just might have a shot.

Besides, she reminded herself, she had a promise to keep.

"Think you can take me somewhere else first?" She asked Askel. "I still need to return the box to Fantas. The only way I know of to see him is by going to see the Mirror Man."

He cocked his head questioningly at her request. "I had thought you weren't comfortable around him," he said finally. "What has changed your mind?"

"I..." she stammered. "I really don't know. But I do know that he is the only one I know of who has a way to get the box back to Fantas, so whether I am comfortable or not, we need to go see the Mirror Man."

Askel reluctantly agreed and they headed to Morgan's house so that she could pick up the box. It wasn't just any box, for it held the Cup of Jamshid, a powerful artifact that Morgan had needed to bargain with Fantas for in order to find a way to defeat the Djieien. In return for letting her use the cup, Fantas had forced Morgan to promise to bring him not only the cup once she was finished but the other items that had allowed her to use the cup in the first place. Those items included a key stolen from the centaur leader and a vial of water she had gotten from the rainbow weavers. The box didn't fit in her satchel with the rest of the items, so she cradled it on her lap as they headed out to see the Mirror Man.

The Mirror Man was an Ancient, one of the most mysterious types of fey. The Ancients were almost impossible to kill, unless one was to uncover their particular weaknesses, each of which was kept as a closely guarded secret. When the Djieien had been sent after her, Morgan had almost been killed repeatedly as she searched for a way to stop it, finally locating its heart and destroying it with the assistance of Askel, Tilson, and a former chosen named Leander.

Unlike the Djieien, the Mirror Man had not lived for thousands or even hundreds of years. He had a normal human lifespan after being born to a human family, inheriting all of the knowledge of his previous incarnations. Morgan still didn't understand why he had been hidden away from both humans and fey in a heavily-guarded tower or why he had been removed from his human family in the first place but that was a matter to deal with later. For now, she just wanted to see him.

The journey to the mountaintop home of the

Mirror Man took hours, most of which Morgan spent napping. She had developed a habit of sleeping on long trips, one which her extended absence from the world of the fey had done little to diminish. She woke with a start as Askel trotted to a stop toward the edge of a grassy field. Small trees and bushes dotted the landscape around a low hill. An opening, marked by shards of crystal growing from it, heralded the entrance to the crystal cavern they needed to pass through in order to reach the Mirror Man.

"It looks the same," Morgan said as she lowered herself to the ground. "Somehow I thought things would look a little different."

"Why would it have changed?" Tilson asked. "It's just a cave. Those don't change very quickly."

"I know," she admitted, "but even the crystals growing from it look the same as they did the last time I was here." She looked at her friends. "I guess it doesn't matter." She hitched her satchel higher onto her shoulder and headed into the cave. Seven months was a long time to be away from their world, at least as far as humans were concerned. She supposed it was a little different in the eyes of the fey, who appeared to have much longer lifespans than her own people did. While she would have hoped to discover that she was missed during her absence, it appeared she wasn't needed for much of anything after all. Not pleased by her own observation, she clutched the box holding the Cup of Jamshid closer to her chest and headed inside.

The cavern was every bit as hot and muggy as she remembered it being. One thing was different from her previous visit, she noted. Where she had been forced to squeeze through a handful of tight openings that were barely large enough for her to pass, now there was enough room for her to maneuver through the spikes of crystal. Even the water that had been flowing across the floor during her previous visit was vastly lower, barely more than a trickle in most places. It still required some contorting to get through all of the formations but she arrived at the dais at the other end of the cavern.

Tilson climbed up to settle himself in the hood of Morgan's sweatshirt, leaving muddy little footprints up the length of her body as he climbed. "What'cha waiting for?" he demanded as he snuggled in. "Let's get going already."

On her first visit to the Mirror Man, a strange creature had greeted her. The creature, likely one of the guardians that watched over all of the Ancients, had taken the appearance of Morgan, only as an undead zombie. While it hadn't done any harm to Morgan and had in fact brought her through the mirror to the waiting lair beyond, seeing herself dead and rotting had shaken Morgan enough that she had experienced nightmares of the encounter for weeks afterward. She scanned the area apprehensively but there was no sign of the guardian. "Something feels wrong," she said finally.

"Like what?" Askel asked from behind them. "It is as you said earlier, everything appears as it was the last time we were here."

"I know that," she admitted, 'but something just feels... different somehow."

"Think it's just because it's been a while since you've been here?" Tilson asked. "Or maybe it's the effects from the Mirror Man."

"Those did cause you some concern before,"

Askel agreed. "Is that the source of your apprehension?"

"No, it's something different." She looked around and realized what was wrong. It had been staring her in the face the whole time. Or rather, she corrected herself, it hadn't. "Where is his guardian?"

The last time Morgan had discovered the guardian of an Ancient missing, the unguarded Ancient had been turned into a golden statue. Fear rising as she thought of the same thing befalling the Mirror Man, she practically sprinted up the remaining stairs and through the reflective surface that served as the boundary between the crystal cavern and the Mirror Man's lair. She reflected back on the myriad times she had thought she'd seen his eyes peering at her, times she had dismissed as imagination. What if, she pushed the idea down even as it occurred to her, they had instead been pleas for help, pleas she had ignored?

The room beyond was the same as she remembered it. The walls were the same stone that was weathering away with age. Papers littered the floor, a couple of which still contained the footprints from her last journey through the room. The table still rested against one wall, complete with a bowl of fruit. Unlike last time, the fresh fruit was now molded and rotten. She eyed everything as she passed, heading directly toward the alcove which held the next passageway. Without a backwards glance, she maneuvered through the mirror and into the dimly-lit room beyond. Fear rising with every step, she jogged across the room and through the open door at the opposite end.

She continued her jog up the seemingly-endless flight of steps which led from the entrance to the courtyard above. Heaving and panting by the time she reached the top, she leaned against the doorframe to catch her breath. It had been a long time since she had run up so many steps. Life in the human world was so much easier, she realized, when there was a helpful elevator or escalator when she needed to ascend or descend from one level to another. In the world of the fey, on the other hand, there were no such conveniences. There were only stairs. So many stairs.

The next time she was left to her own devices

for an extended period of time, she decided, she would spend a little less time moping and wondering when they would call for her and a little more time working on her endurance training. A year ago, running all of those stairs would have barely winded her. Now, she felt like her legs were on fire.

In the courtyard, the massive tree with spears for leaves waited, appearing almost exactly as it had the last time Morgan had been there. The mists swirled around it, keeping her from taking a close examination but its branches poked through the fog, granting her and Tilson a clear view of the tips of its branches.

"Come on," she said, more to herself than to anyone else. She scanned the skies, searching for any sight of the massive bird that had attacked her the first time she had crossed the courtyard. "If that thing sees us, we'll be eaten for sure."

"What thing?" Tilson's eyes followed her gaze, searching the skies. "I don't see anything up there."

"Neither do I," she agreed. "I don't see anything at all." Even the small songbirds that were everywhere in the world of the fey were conspicuously absent. "That doesn't exactly make me feel any better." First the zombie guardian was missing, she realized, now the roc was gone. What had happened to all of the Mirror Man's guardians?

Growing more concerned by the step, she hurried across the courtyard where a door, identical to the one through which they had just come, waited. She twisted the knob and shouldered the door open, barely slowing as she moved, and arrived inside with no resistance. She tripped through the entrance, surprised that the door had opened so easily.

"What the heck is going on?" she asked as she closed the door behind them. Just because the roc hadn't made an appearance, that didn't mean that it was gone completely. While she doubted its ability to squeeze through the narrow doorway, she wasn't willing to take any chances. "Mirror Man?" she called out as she stepped further into the room. "It's Morgan, Morgan Lafayette. Are you here?"

"And Tilson, too," the haltija called out from his perch in her hood.

She wasn't surprised to receive no answer in return. Although she had hoped that her growing suspicions were wrong, that she would find the Mirror Man safe and secure in his home, a deeper part of her had already known what to expect. All she still needed to do, much as she didn't want to, was to find what was left of him.

"Is he a statue, like those people back in town?" she wondered, half to Tilson and half to herself as she walked from room to room, searching for any sign of what had happened to her friend. "Or did he get turned into gold like Amahté-Baki?"

"I doubt he was turned to stone," Tilson said. "The Ancients are hard to kill, you remember what Corran said while we were trying to find a way to defeat the spider. Since the Mirror Man's an Ancient, that probably means he wouldn't fall for a trick like that."

"That's true," she admitted, "but he still could be. Corran said that he didn't have any idea of what was doing this to people, which means it could be something powerful enough to turn even an Ancient to stone."

"Well, let's just take the box back to Fantas

so we can get out of here," he grumbled. "I don't like it in this place, there are too many mirrors all over the place."

She could understand his discomfort. Almost every wall of the Mirror Man's lair was covered with an assortment of mirrors, each of which reflected their images back to them to form a strangely kaleidoscopic vision, like a funhouse mirror only with a lot more images. Hundreds, if not thousands, of Morgans and Tilsons watched them with curiosity as they examined the remaining rooms, finally admitting defeat when there was no sign of the lair's owner.

"C'mon, Morgan," Tilson tugged on her earlobe. "It's why we came here, isn't it?"

"Yeah," she agreed, "but without the Mirror Man, I don't know how to open the portal to Fantas."

"Well, that's a fine problem you've caused for us, then. Why did we come all the way out here, lugging that huge box all over the place, if you didn't even know how to get to where you were headed?"

"I wasn't exactly expecting the Mirror Man to be missing, you know. Magicgleam said that he was always here, so why would I expect him to be gone?"

"How should I know," the haltija's voice became higher with agitation. "Maybe you should just ask her where he's gone off to."

"That's not a bad idea." The more Morgan thought about it, the more merit his suggestion had. "She's the one who told me how to find him in the first place, maybe she knows how to find him now."

As they made their way back out to meet back up with Askel, Morgan pondered every idea she could come up with for why the Mirror Man had been gone. Maybe, she realized, he actually had a lot of lairs and moved among them, just as how humans occasionally moved from one house to another, or like a vacation home. If he had simply relocated, she realized, that could also explain where his guardians had gone. He had probably just taken them along with him when he moved. But if that was the case, why hadn't he taken any of his belongings with him?

She was still disappointed that she hadn't been able to see him yet. Although she hadn't said anything about it to her friends, she had been looking forward to the opportunity to see him again. The intense reaction she had experienced the last time she met up with the Mirror Man had long since faded but she wondered if it would happen again the next time she saw him.

"What do you mean, he's not there?" Askel asked when they emerged from the crystal cavern, box still in hand. "What happened to him?"

"We're not sure," Morgan said as she heaved herself onto his back. "We're hoping Magicgleam can have some answers on that. Think you can take us to see her?"

"Yes, I can do that." Once she and Tilson were settled, he jogged a few paces to get up enough speed to take flight. "It is unusual for him to be gone," he explained as they flew. "Perhaps Bas-Grann found him, just as he found Amahté-Baki."

"I hope not," Morgan said. "At least, I didn't find any statues of him, golden or otherwise." Despite her words, she was concerned. The Council of Fey still hadn't come across any means of returning Amahté-Baki to her natural state and Morgan didn't want to even imagine the same fate befalling the Mirror Man. Just how many of her friends was she going to lose to that horrible man?

MAGICGLEAM AND STORMSHOCK

They landed on the edge of a massive meadow on Halkirk Island. Just to their south, a mountain of boulders waited, hidden remnants of the path that led to Magicgleam's lair. The stones were more than just a pile of rubble, despite their current appearance. Each of the stones was a pillar that, when upright, soared into the sky overhead. At that moment, the gateway was closed and the boulders were scattered across the ground in a rough circle, silent and waiting.

While Morgan had been to the island on a few

occasions previously, she had yet to uncover the means by which Askel was able to activate the portal. As he did every time, he led them into the center of the ring of fallen stones and wrapped his wings around Morgan and Tilson. The world shifted and turned inside-out and upside-down in a now-familiar way as the magical portal activated. When Askel released them, they stood upon the fully restored stone walkway that led directly to the secretive dragon's lair. Unwilling to wait, Morgan strode purposefully across the stones.

"Well, well, well," Magicgleam's voice called to them as soon as they entered her cave. "If it isn't the chosen. To what do I owe the honor of a visit?"

"We're here about the Mirror Man," Morgan explained. As usual, she was unable to spot the dragon in the dimly-lit cavern, so well was Magicgleam able to blend into her surroundings.

"I've already told you how to find him," Magicgleam said as the wall rippled before the trio and the massive dragon began to take shape. "Don't tell me you've forgotten the way already. I had believed you to be more retentive than that."

"No, we haven't forgotten how to find him." Morgan stepped closer as she spoke. "In fact, we just came from there. You see, he's missing."

"Missing?" The dragon's eyebrow ridge rose in surprise and she reared up, the top of her head almost scraping against the cavern's ceiling. "What do you mean he is missing?"

"He wasn't there," Tilson supplied. "We went to see him so we could find Fantas again, but he was gone. No Mirror Man, not even a note to say when he'd be back."

"We're worried about him," Morgan explained. "We had figured he would be safe, since his place is so well hidden, but with him being gone and nobody seems to know where he is, we're worried that something bad may have happened to him."

"We hoped you would have some idea of where he could be found," Askel added. "Because you are the one who is closest to him, we thought he may have told you where he went."

Magicgleam's head lowered until she was practically eye-to-eye with her small group of visitors, or at least as close to such as she could manage with her immense bulk. She peered from one to the next until her gaze finally settled on Morgan. "I had been unaware of this," she finally admitted as she returned to her original position. "This news distresses and concerns me as well, as this is the first time in my lifetime that the Mirror Man has not been precisely where he is supposed to be."

"In your lifetime?" Morgan wondered aloud. "I thought he was basically human, with a human lifespan. How could you know where he has been for your whole lifetime?"

"That is true," the dragon agreed. "He lives a mortal life. However, he incarnates immediately upon death and I am able to track him as soon as he is reborn. As such, I always know where he is."

Morgan hadn't known that Magicgleam could track him that way from lifetime to lifetime. That reincarnation ability with the retention of his memories from one life to the next was the magic that caused him to be regarded as an Ancient, despite having a relatively short existence for each of his incarnations. "If you can tell where he is as soon as he is born," she asked, "does that mean you have a way to track him now?" If Magicgleam had some way of finding where the Mirror Man was, that would be a big relief – and a big help. Maybe she could even tell them where to find him.

"I do not," Magicgleam admitted. "The means by which I track him from death to birth involve following his ethereal trail to ascertain to where his essence is transferred. Without that, I have no means of determining his whereabouts."

"Well, that is information of a sort," Askel pointed out. When Morgan looked at him quizzically, he explained. "If Magicgleam can tell where he is when he transfers from one body to the next, she would know if that had happened." He looked between Morgan and Magicgleam. "If you have not determined that he is moving to a new form, that means he is still alive."

"That's right," Tilson jumped up and down on Morgan's shoulder. "That's true, so that's actually really good news. Wherever he is, we know he's alive."

"True," Morgan agreed slowly, "it's better than nothing but I'm still pretty concerned. If something happened to him like what happened to Amahté-Baki, would that end up resulting in an ether transfer? Or would his ether just be trapped in a gold statue like hers?" Much as she didn't want to think about the possibility of something killing the Mirror Man, the idea of something locking his essence and trapping him for an eternity sounded much, much worse.

Although she had been strangely uncomfortable the first time she had met the Mirror Man, after just a short period of time that feeling had faded. Askel had explained that she had fallen under his magic, an aura that surrounds him and causes almost everyone to react similarly upon first encountering him. She was curious as to whether she would feel normally the next time she met him, or whether the time that had elapsed since their previous meeting would cause her to react once more. Beyond that, she genuinely liked him, although she still didn't understand why. He was a strange boy, but he was one of the only humans she had met in her service to the fey.

Considering he was also an Ancient, she wasn't really sure whether she should consider him as a boy or a fey but he was born and lived the lifespan of a human, so that should count for something, right?

"There is one other thing before you leave," Magicgleam called out to her. "As I understand things, you have not received your magical training yet, is that correct?"

"Yeah," Morgan responded sullenly. She had only recently discovered that all of the chosen before her had been trained in magic before being sent out into the dangerous situations she constantly found herself in. For some reason, Corran had decided that she needed no such training. She didn't particularly like his decision, as magic sounded fascinating to her, but there was little she could do about it. She had one spell book, stolen from a pyramid in Egypt, but she only knew how to use one spell from it.

"I think that it is high time you started."

Morgan's brows shot up and she took an involuntary step closer to the reflective dragon. "What?" she asked, certain she had misunderstood.

"You heard me, chosen," Magicgleam lowered her head to look Morgan square in the eye. "I will make the necessary arrangements to have your training begin as soon as possible."

"But..." Morgan searched for the words to express how she felt at that. The elvor who spoke for the council had been clear that she was not to receive this training, had something happened to change his mind? "What about Corran?"

"Leave the elvor to me," Magicgleam re-assured her. "This is no longer his decision, it is mine." She blinked her massive eye and Morgan realized with a start that she could see her entire reflection in one pupil. "You realize, don't you, that this will likely cause additional problems for you? The council at Zea Island answers to Corran and the fey have never gone against his wishes. This will likely cause ripples among them."

"I want magic." Morgan's words were quiet but the meaning was clear. She had never been more certain of anything in her life. Although she had magical items and trinkets to do many of the things required of her, she had spent years fantasizing about what it would be like to have that kind of ability on her own. Even before she had been selected as a chosen, Morgan had been fascinated by all things magical. That had only compounded the disappointment she had felt at Corran's decree that she would not be taught and she had sulked for days afterwards. Now, she no longer cared whether her training upset some of the fey. She wanted to learn.

There were more words, but Morgan heard none of them. She was going to be trained in magic after all? Despite Corran's objections? She hadn't been aware that Magicgleam could overrule the elvor's decision like that but she wasn't about to argue against the decision of the dragon.

As Askel guided her and Tilson back outside, Morgan could swear she heard Magicgleam's voice one last time, echoing out of the cavern, "goodness knows you are going to need it before you are done." She jerked around to ask for more information but the cavern was empty. The dragon had once again disappeared.

There was another, more secret reason why she was pleased that Magicgleam had decided she needed to learn magic despite Corran. Although she hadn't expressed as much to anyone,

Morgan was beginning to believe that Corran was not as trustworthy as she had initially believed him to be. Perhaps she had just been too trusting, too willing to accept that these magical creatures were all honest, but her time as a chosen had taught her otherwise. Just because someone was fey, that didn't mean that they could, or should, be trusted. Loathe as she was to believe the worst of someone she considered a friend, there had been too many things she had seen or heard that led her to believe that something was not as it should be with Corran.

And she did still consider the elvor to be a friend, despite her distrust. She liked the elvor every bit as much that day as she had in the days before he had lost her trust, a loss that he was as-yet unaware of. But there was definitely something amiss with her friend and though she couldn't put her finger on precisely what, she knew that he had lied to her in the past, possibly on multiple occasions. With no clue about what his end game may be, all Morgan could do was to continue acting the part of the dutiful, more-or-less obedient chosen and wait to see what happened.

If it turned out to be something bad, as things were more likely to turn out in her experience so far, she felt that knowledge of magic might just be what she needed. Preparation was key and when it came to the fey, she needed to be as prepared as she possibly could be.

They had been flying for some time before she realized that they were headed in the wrong direction. Instead of heading directly back to Zea Island, or even to her home as she had expected, they were headed in the opposite direction. The sun, which should have been on her left side, was on her right. She blinked around in confusion, not recognizing where they were or how long they had been flying. "Where are we?" she finally asked. "Aren't we heading back to Zea Island?"

"Not quite yet," Askel responded. "There is one other person with whom we can check to see if there has been any word of the Mirror Man."

"Who?"

"Stormshock, of course," the gryphon laughed. "Even if he doesn't know what has befallen the Mirror Man, he may have some ideas on what has happened to Amahté-Baki and how to return the statues in your world back to life."

"How much further to his grove?"

"Not much, it's just beyond the next mountains."

Morgan settled back once more, pleased that she would get to see Stormshock so soon. The great green dragon had become one of her first friends in the world of the fey, despite how afraid she had initially been when meeting him for the first time. A short time ago, he had made it appear that he had been killed and Morgan had been nearly overcome with grief at the loss. When he had resurfaced and she learned he still lived, her relief had been almost as great as her initial sorrow. His continued existence was still a secret to most of the fey, as the person responsible for the deaths of so many dragons still hadn't been uncovered. For as long as he remained in danger, he would remain in hiding. Pleased as she was at finally learning the truth, Morgan was determined to do everything she could to keep his secret safe.

After they landed in the familiar clearing that Stormshock called home and exchanged greetings, Askel got to the point of their visit and inquired about the missing Mirror Man.

"You need not worry about him," Stormshock reassured them. "He is safe. Since the fey have been under constant threat, particularly now that Morgan has confirmed his existence, the High Council has decided that he should be further hidden as well to ensure his safety."

The news was reassuring to Morgan but she couldn't help feeling a pang of disappointment. If the Mirror Man had been moved to a more secure hiding place, that could only mean that she wouldn't get the opportunity to see him again.

"There is no reason to worry," Stormshock interrupted her thoughts. "You will see him again soon enough, of that I am certain."

Morgan's cheeks reddened as she realized her reaction must have been much more visible than she had expected. "It's not like that," she protested. "I was supposed to bring the Cup of Jamshid back to Fantas, but the only way I have to get to him is with the help of the Mirror Man. I don't know where Fantas's lair is."

Stormshock chuckled. "Do not worry about

that either. Fantas is quite upset that the return of his Cup has been delayed, as he is well aware that the Cup has already been activated and the Djieien destroyed, but he now understands the situation in much clearer detail. But since you currently have no way to return the items to Fantas, which is obviously weighing heavily on your heart, I am willing to assist on that. Leave the items with me and I will see that they are safely returned to him."

Reluctantly, but not seeing any real reason to object, she set the box containing the promised items onto the rocks next to Stormshock's pool. The dragon was the second to make such an offer but, unlike the last time the offer had been made, her medallion gave her no indication of trickery and lies. At least this time she could be sure that the box would be delivered and her promise would be kept, even if she wasn't to be the one personally delivering on it.

Other discussions soon followed which kept Morgan's interest, at least in part. One of the primary reasons for Stormshock's continued hiding was due to the possibility of a traitor within the Council. This wasn't news to Morgan, as she and Stormshock had already discussed just such a possibility. She wondered whether the dragon suspected Corran just as she herself did and considered asking him directly but thought better of it. He wasn't likely to answer on his suspicions until he was more informed and she didn't want to accidentally focus his attention on the wrong person, should her concerns be unfounded. Until she was more certain of her suspicions, she would continue to hold her tongue.

There had been no further evidence about the traitor or traitors – for there was no reason to believe there was only one – within the Council. "Other Councils have begun to have similar suspicions," Askel added. "They are becoming wary of their own members as well."

This was news to Morgan, and surprising news at that. "How do we know about this?" she asked. She had known that there were many other councils besides the one she worked with. She had even worked with members of other councils to solve one problem or another. This was the first time she had heard even the slightest mention of a traitor in other councils.

If that was the case, then the problem must be much more widespread than she had originally believed it to have been. Ameil Bas-Grann continued to gain ground in the battle between himself and the fey and she was still unable to come up with a means by which he could be stopped. At the rate things were going, she wasn't altogether certain that the side she represented would emerge victorious.

"They have petitioned the High Council for assistance."

"So what are we doing about it?"

Askel shrugged, an odd-looking sight on the gryphon. "At this point, until we have more information, there is very little we can do."

Morgan scowled although she agreed with her friend's assessment. All they had been able to do from the very beginning had been in reaction to Bas-Grann's schemes. Without understanding what his actual end game was, it was highly unlikely that they would be able to do anything about his ultimate plot.

~ 5 ~

CATS

They continued discussing a bit longer, eventually turning to the topic of the stone statues that had begun appearing with much more frequency. Morgan explained about the humans being turned into statues that she had uncovered in her world, along with the statues of fey she had found.

"This is serious indeed," Stormshock admitted once she finished her explanation. "It is highly unusual for any magical changes such as that to impact both humans and fey." He looked thoughtful for a long moment before asking, "have you heard of this happening elsewhere?"

"I'm not sure," Morgan answered. "I hadn't really been paying a lot of attention but I don't remember hearing anything specifically about it. No news reports about a lot of people disappearing or anything like that. If I hadn't spotted the statue I did, I probably still wouldn't have known anything about any of this. All of this only happened shortly before Corran called for me."

Stormshock nodded. "I see. What about among the fey? Have any of them reported similar incidents?"

Askel shook his feathered head. "We have some reports but not many as of yet. That was another reason we were hoping to contact the Mirror Man, so that he could help us reach others and find out if they have experienced similar incidents."

"Of the reports you have received, how many of them have theories on how this is happening? How are the fey reacting to these events?"

"Nobody seems to know what is causing them yet," Askel admitted. "Everyone is becoming desperate for information, anything that will help to protect them from being turned to stone as well, but I have heard no ideas on the source of the problem."

"Should we contact the other Councils?" Morgan asked. "I'm sure there has to be another way to contact them other than by finding the Mirror Man, so maybe we should start reaching out to them directly." She looked among her friends and added, "they might know something about what's going on and have an idea on how to stop it. At the very least, we should probably start letting people know this is happening so that they can do whatever they can to protect themselves from being turned to stone as well."

"The idea has merit," Askel agreed. "My information has only come from what had been brought to me, I do not believe any have gone to seek the information directly."

"There is little we can do to warn the humans but perhaps spreading word among the fey could prove useful." Stormshock settled into his pool. "Go to see the cats, I believe you already have a relationship with some of them. See what they know, if they know anything, and warn them that they could be targeted as well."

Needing no further instruction, the trio of Morgan, Askel, and Tilson headed out of the clearing. As Askel took a running start to lift into the air, Morgan could have kicked herself for not having thought of her friends among the cat tribe until now. It hadn't been very long ago when Tekli, one of the cats, had come to her rescue when she had badly needed assistance. To know that he could have in turn needed her assistance and she hadn't been there to help was upsetting, at the very least.

She spent the entire flight worried about her feline friends, wondering whether she would find them safe when she arrived or whether they would be stone statues. She couldn't even quite imagine how she would react if she discovered the attacks had reached them as well; the idea of losing more of her friends was simply too horrible to bear. Was that the reason Tekli hadn't been by to visit for so long?

She couldn't help but wonder if this had been how the dragons felt when they had been under attack, an attack that had taken almost all of the dragons as its victims. That attack had been what brought her to become a chosen and had introduced her to the new world which now felt more like home than her own world did. It had also introduced her to Tilson and Askel, as well as the rest of the fey, people she could no longer see life without. Strange to think that all of the new experiences she had been involved with had all started because of a widespread scheme like that.

She wondered if the dragons had been as afraid when the attacks had started as they were when the attacks stopped, if they had realized somehow that it had been the beginning of the end for their species. While there were still dragons left among the fey, the once-rare breed had become almost extinct. Leander, the former chosen who had been accused of the attacks, was now one of her closest allies and, not for the first time, she wondered who had actually been responsible. She had her own belief that somehow Bas-Grann had masterminded the plot but had neither seen nor heard anything to support that belief. Even without proof, it sounded like something the horrid man would devise.

She let out a sound that was part sigh of relief and part groan of concern as the gryphon circled, looking for a place to land. "Where do you want to start?" he asked over his shoulder.

"I would like to start with the Irusan, if that's okay." The Irusan was the leader of the tribe of cats, whom Morgan had only met once previously. The enormous tiger had scared her during their first meeting but it had ended well and Morgan now thought of the entire tribe as her friends. Assuming that the cats had not been afflicted by the stoning, she hoped that he may have some ideas on what was behind the attacks. If he didn't know what was behind them, perhaps he would know of a way to either stop them from occurring again or to return those who had been turned to stone back into flesh. She had learned that the cats often knew things that they didn't willingly share with the rest of the fey. As chosen, she seemed to be an exception to their reluctance.

"I cannot go directly to the home of the Irusan," Askel explained, "but I can take you to the clearing where the rest of the cats can be found. One of them will have to bring you the rest of the way."

"Assuming they're all still alive," Tilson said

quietly, running his tiny hands over the puff of fur on the tip of his tail. "We don't really know how far this has spread, do we?"

"Don't say things like that," Morgan admonished him. "Hopefully it won't be a problem, us dropping in unannounced like this." Once Askel jogged to a stop on the ground, she slid from his back, gathered her belongings, and waited for Tilson to take his customary place on her shoulder. Despite her response, she had to agree with Tilson. The haltija had only said what all of them had been thinking, although neither she nor Askel had been brave enough to say the words aloud. When he was settled and ready as well, she headed into the clearing in search of the tribe.

She didn't make it very far across the clearing before she was accosted by a pair of cubs. They were the size of large house cats, except for their enormous ears. Most of their bodies were covered with tawny fur, except for their black ears and a pair of thin black strips that bordered the area from inner eye to nose. The pair came bounding toward Morgan, growling and snarling. She stopped moving at their approach and they stopped, almost completely in unison, only a few paces away from her.

One sat fully erect, eyes wide and unblinking as it regarded the intruders. The other sat just to the right of the first, head lowered warily, curiously glancing from Morgan to Tilson and then over to Askel before returning back to regard Morgan once more.

"Hey, guys," she said quietly, keeping her voice calm and even. "We're not here to hurt you, we just want to speak with your tribe members." Even as she spoke, she wondered whether the cubs could understand her. She was wearing the amulet that allowed her to communicate with both fey and animals, but she had no idea whether there was an age at which the cubs would be able to understand her. This was her first experience with young fey of any kind and she was at a loss on how to continue.

"Morgan!" A massive panther walked out of the trees. "How wonderful to see you again."

Morgan smiled reflexively as she recognized her dear friend. "Tekli, I'm so glad to see you!" She ran to the panther and hugged him. "I was so worried about you guys."

"Worried? What have you been worried about?"

"A lot of people, both human and fey, have been turned into stone and I thought maybe that had happened to you, too. We're here to speak with the Irusan at the very least but I would like to be able to speak with the Oracle as well. We're hoping they have some ideas on what's going on."

Tekli nodded sagely. "I had heard about that. Thankfully, none of us have been afflicted by whatever has been causing this. Is the Irusan expecting you?"

She shook her head. "I don't think so. I was sent here by..." unsure about how widespread knowledge of Stormshock's survival was, she hesitated before continuing, "members of the council. I don't know whether they were in communication with any of your tribe or not."

Tekli nodded. "Regardless, I am certain that he will be pleased to see you."

"Can you bring me to him? Askel says that it needs to be a member of the tribe."

"I can, indeed. Let me bring these two cubs back to the rest of the tribe and I will return momentarily." He turned to herd the pair of cubs, who had crept closer during the conversation. "Come now, let's get you back where you belong. You know your mother dislikes it when you wander off on your own like this."

Morgan waited with Askel and Tilson for his return. As she had the last time traveling with Tekli, she rode on his back as they flew through the trees. The speeds at which the panther was able to travel, never missing a step, were impressive. Cats were known for sure-footedness and Tekli was no exception.

Before long, they found themselves at the edge of the lake. Just as it had the last time Morgan had been there, the Irusan's house impressed. It waited in the lake, accessed only by a narrow wooden walkway. She dropped off of Tekli's back and squished into the muddy shore.

The torches that marked the entrance to the Irusan's building were lit, just as they had been previously. Morgan wondered whether they had a fuel source to cause the fires or whether they burned by magical means. "I'll be back soon," she promised the panther as she stepped from the muddy ground onto the wooden bridge.

Boards creaked and swayed beneath her feet on the gentle waves and she was careful to walk down the center of the bridge. Although the motion was nowhere near enough to knock her off and she knew how to swim should she fall anyway, she still wasn't interested in seeing how deep the water there was.

Just as she reached the far end, where the pitched roof of the Irusan's home waited, a shadow fell across the entryway, blocking the light from within and causing Morgan to take an involuntary step backwards. Just because she had been welcomed the last time she had been there, that didn't automatically mean that she would be equally welcomed this time. She just hoped that the Irusan was in a good mood... and not hungry.

The massive tiger stepped out of the building, enormous paws steady on the creaking surface. "Greetings, chosen. What brings you to my home?"

Morgan cast a glance over her shoulder, weighing the distance between herself and the shore. Deciding that Tekli was far enough away, she spoke quietly. "Stormshock sent me."

He nodded his head sagely. "I was expecting something similar to this. We have been hearing tell of some strange happenings, both in our world and in yours."

"Yeah," she agreed. "It's gotten pretty bad out there. People are being turned into stone all over the place and we haven't got any idea how it's happening. That's actually why I'm here. I wanted to check on you guys and Stormshock wanted me to see if you had heard of anything to turn them back to the way they're supposed to be, or if you knew of any way to stop it from happening in the first place."

"Come inside." He turned gracefully and stepped back into the interior of the building. Morgan followed him inside, blinking back tears as she did. For some reason, the more she talked about what was happening, the more she felt the loss of those who had been turned to stone.

"None of my cats have yet succumbed to this affliction," he explained once they were both safely inside. "We have been staying close in the hopes of preventing just such an occurrence."

That explained why she hadn't seen much of Tekli lately. Morgan's hopes fell. She had expected the tiger to have at least some ideas that would help her. "But do you know of any way to reverse the process?"

"Of that, I am unaware. Perhaps the Oracle will have better information than what I know." He regarded her with wise eyes. "Because we have stayed close to our lands, we are perhaps not as aware as you are of what has been going on. Please, enlighten me."

Morgan took a deep breath, eyes closed as she willed herself to stay calm. "First, the people in my world started being turned into stone. Things like that aren't supposed to happen in the human world." She lowered her eyes and glanced around the room without looking at much in particular. "But it's not just in the human world, it's happening to the fey too. Even the Amahté-Baki became a statue. Like, a for-real statue, not just looking like a statue like she appeared the first time I saw her.

"Even the Mirror Man is gone. Magicgleam said she'd never even heard of him leaving his place, so nobody knows where he's gone off to or if he's a statue somewhere too. Stormshock said he's okay somewhere but until I see him, I can't quite believe it." She raised her eyes up to look at the Irusan's face. "I'm really happy that none of you got turned too, I was a bit afraid that when I got here, there wouldn't be anything left but statues."

"I can understand your concern and I appreciate your worry for my tribe." He stepped closer and nudged her with his muzzle, whiskers tickling her ear as he did. "We are all saddened by the loss of the Ancient, and the disappearance of the Mirror Man is disturbing news to us as well. But rest assured that we are safe, there is nothing for you to worry about us at this moment." He leveled one wise golden eye at her in silence as she wiped a tear away.

She was quickly running out of people to ask for assistance. If the Oracle didn't have anything more than the Irusan did, that would mean she wouldn't be able to help her people, the people of either of the worlds she inhabited. "I'll go and speak with the Oracle next," she finally said.

"He will be pleased to see you," the Irusan smiled. "It had been a long time since the chosen has grown so close to our tribe, so it is nice to have that relationship once more."

Once she had herself back under control, she headed out to meet up with Tekli. If the panther noticed her reddened eyes, he was kind enough to make no mention of it as she climbed onto his back and they headed further up the shoreline.

The scenery blurred past as Tekli ran, the buffeting wind giving Morgan more than enough of an excuse to wipe her eyes once more when they stopped. She looked around as she climbed down again, just as amazed at the scene as she had been the last time she had been to see the Oracle.

The pool next to the Oracle's platform had deepened and widened since Morgan's last visit, so that she had to jump over a narrow strip of water in order to reach the stone stairs. She stopped at the bottom of the staircase before proceeding up, watching in delight as the fireflies danced to their own silent music. In some ways, they reminded her of the peri she had watched through her classroom window.

"You enjoyed watching them dance the last time you were here as well," a deep voice called from the top of the platform. "It is nice to see that at least some things do not change." The head of an enormous white tiger peered over the edge of the platform, regarding Morgan with an eye the color of the crystalline water that surrounded them.

Even had she wanted to, Morgan couldn't hold back the smile at seeing his face. "You have no idea how glad I am to see you," she explained as she climbed the rest of the stairs. "The Irusan said that you were okay, that you hadn't been turned to stone, but I couldn't just believe it until I saw for myself."

"An understandable concern," he smiled at her arrival, wickedly sharp fangs only barely visible. "We had many of the same fears about you as well. In fact, I believe Tekli had been petitioning to check on your well-being himself."

"I didn't know that." She glanced back to the shore where her friend waited. "He didn't say anything."

"Nor would he, as it is clearly evident that you are exactly as you should be." He pushed himself to a seated position, his head still even with Morgan's own. "Come, then. I understand you are on a mission of some importance, as always. How can we be of assistance?"

"I'm sure you know that people – humans and fey – are being turned to stone?" When he nodded, she continued. "I am here to see if you know of any way to reverse it, to put them back the way they were."

The Oracle blinked slowly at her before responding. "I understand your concern and your reasons for coming to me with this request. Unfortunately, I know of no way to reverse petrification once it has occurred."

"Petrification?" she asked, rolling the unfamiliar word around on her tongue. "Is that what it's called?" She knew that there was a natural process that would result in things being petrified over thousands of years, but she had dismissed the possibility long ago. Now, it seemed, the fey used the same word for the current attacks.

"Indeed it is. We know of very few beings capable of doing such a thing and have identified none of them that could be responsible. Our tribe had hoped for the same as you, that we could uncover some means of restoring those who had been afflicted but so far, we have nothing to offer."

Morgan's heart sank at his words, her smile falling as he spoke. "So you don't know either?"

"We are still searching," he reassured her. "As soon as we know anything about the source of this atrocity or means of restoring from it, we will send word to you immediately. I am certain that Tekli would be willing to bring news to you, if none of the others are able to do so."

$$\sim 6 \sim$$

NATHAN

Although Morgan wanted to continue hunting for answers, seeking information anywhere it could be found, Corran insisted that there was nothing more for her to do until his inquiries began turning up new leads, so once again she was sent back home. Home was the last place she wanted to be, as her friends were still in danger and she badly wanted to find a way to stop the petrification attacks, but there was little room to argue. She spent the trip back to her house in sullen silence, refusing to even respond to Askel's well-meaning attempts to cheer her up.

She was still in a foul mood when she woke the following morning, scowling at her alarm clock. The alarm had done nothing wrong, it simply announced that she needed to wake in order to get to school on time. Unimpressed with its insistence, Morgan slapped the button to allow her five more minutes of peaceful quiet and settled back against her pillows.

"Morgan, honey, come get breakfast." Her mother's voice called from beyond her closed bedroom door. She groaned in response, knowing that whatever her mother made, it was sure to be inedible. For all her the woman's talents, cooking was not among them.

Recognizing that she had no other options, she climbed out of bed and went in search of clothes. Liore, the shapeshifting elvor who stood in for Morgan in the human world while she was working with the fey, had done a much better job lately of keeping at least one or two sets of clean clothes on hand for Morgan's return. The first handful of times Morgan had been gone for an extended absence, Liore had left her with almost nothing to wear upon her return, requiring Morgan to do laundry no matter how tired she was. Since then, the girls had come up with a reasonable system, in which Liore kept two sets of clothing clean and ready for Morgan to wear.

Liore and Morgan also shared a notebook which was kept on Morgan's desk. In this note-book, they both wrote the events of each day and any important information that might be needed, such as school gossip, family meetings, and any upcoming homework or tests. While reading the notes from her absence, Morgan was relived to discover that she had just missed a test in one of her classes. Hopefully Liore had done well on it, because Morgan certainly wouldn't have. One thing that was decidedly lacking while she was out in the world of the fey was any time to catch up on her studies.

"If you want a ride to school," her mother's voice called again, "you had better hurry. Your father is leaving in fifteen minutes."

"I'm coming," she called down in response. She had no objection to walking to school, but she rarely saw her father and the chance to spend a little bit of time with him was more than she was willing to pass up. Less than five minutes later, she scuttled down the stairs to catch up with him before he left. She picked up a pair of pancakes from the stack on the table, hoping they were safe to consume, and followed him out to his car.

Morgan had always been close to her father but recent events had made her realize just how close they were. Only a short period of time ago, an evil magus named Ameil Bas-Grann had broken into her home and attacked her in her sleep. Tekli the panther had come to her rescue and she and her family had been brought to Zea Island for everyone's safety. While there, she had learned that her father had once been a chosen just as she was, his memories erased when he entered adulthood. He had requested to not have his memories erased again, which Corran had agreed to, but there had been no discussion about it since then. Much as Morgan wanted to know whether he had retained his memories after all, she didn't want to risk seeming foolish if they had been erased. She knew that her mother's memories had been erased, as that fact had quickly become apparent with general conversation, but her father remained a mystery.

At the same time, she had also discovered that the fact her father had once been a chosen was the very reason that she herself had been selected to become one. There was something in her bloodline, something passed down through the generations from parent to child, that the fey depended on.

"You've sure got a lot on your mind this morning," her father smiled over at her as he backed the little silver car out of the driveway. "Anything you want to share?"

Morgan looked up at him in surprise, wondering if he had somehow heard her thoughts. "I, umm..." she stammered, unsure of where to begin, or whether she even should. Should she just ask him? How would he react if his memories had been erased and she started talking about another world? After only a moment or two, she decided not to pursue the idea. Instead, she decided on a different topic of conversation. "I'm worried about a friend."

That much was true. As curious as she was about her father and her lineage, she was more concerned about what had happened to the Mirror Man. "I met him a little while ago but when I tried to talk with him the other day, he was nowhere to be found. Nobody seems to know where he's gone."

Her father raised an eyebrow at that. "Do you think he's in danger? Or do you think he ran away from home?"

She hadn't considered the possibility that the Mirror Man had left voluntarily. From everything she had been told, that was highly unlikely. "I really don't know," she admitted. "But everyone I've spoken with seems to think it's really strange that he's not home anymore." She wasn't about to admit that the mutual friends she referred to were dragons and other fey but she hoped her father wouldn't ask too many prying questions.

"Maybe he's just on vacation, lots of families do that this time of year."

She should have known that the conversation wouldn't go anywhere. There wasn't any way that her father could understand why she was so concerned or why it was strange that the Mirror Man had disappeared. As far as he knew, her friend was just another schoolmate who lived at home with his parents. "Maybe you're right," she said quietly as she turned to look out the window.

Thankfully, they spent the rest of the trip in silence. She wasn't sure how she could handle any more of her father's questions right then without sounding like a crazy person. A dragon had told her that the Mirror Man never left home but how could she explain that to the human driving the car? And how could she explain that the Mirror Man wasn't a human, at least not really. He was an Ancient, a special creature that was both human and fey, part of both worlds and yet also not a part of either. His home was a castle with strange trees in the courtyard, mirrors on all the walls, and an enormous bird that had tried to kill her the first time she had been to see him.

When they stopped in front of her school, she opened the door and stepped out. Before walking away, however, she turned and leaned down to look at her father through the open car door. "Be careful, okay? I don't want anything bad to happen to you."

He smiled at that. "I think that's what I'm supposed to be saying to you."

"How about we both be careful, then?"

"I think I can live with that. Have a good day today, okay?"

As he drove off, she headed up the walk toward the school, backpack over one shoulder. It felt different carrying the backpack than it did carrying her satchel and she wished she had a single-strap bag for school to make it a little more comfortable. She trudged down the orange and brown checkerboard patterned hallway to her class and settled into her usual seat. The whole school felt foreign to her, which wasn't surprising considering how little time she spent there. She may have a good attendance record but that was more due to the regular appearances by Liore than her own attendance.

"...seriously hot. I wonder where he's from?"

"I don't know. He looks European though, doesn't he?"

Morgan tried to ignore the inane chatter, which proved impossible as the pair of girls seated near her both turned to look at her expectantly. Blinking between them, she racked her brain to figure out what they were waiting for and, for that matter, who they were. "Who?" she asked finally, admitting defeat.

"The new guy," one of the girls, a tall girl with shiny blond hair that was pulled back in a high ponytail answered, her voice incredulous. "Don't tell me you hadn't heard about him."

"Of course she didn't notice, Rebecca," the second girl added. "This is Morgan we're talking about. She's more interested in video games than boys."

The name Rebecca called forth a memory from Morgan's mind. Liore had mentioned these girls, Rebecca and Stacy, in their shared notebook. She had developed a friendship with them while Morgan had been gone. She groaned internally at the realization; the last thing she needed was to spend an entire day talking with girls she didn't know about boys she didn't know. Not for the first time, she wondered how all of the other chosen had managed to lead two lives at the same time and not go crazy trying to keep up with both.

"I saw him in the office earlier this week," Stacy supplied. "He was getting registered and I heard them say that he is supposed to be starting today."

"I saw him too," Rebecca added. "At about the same time. I think he was leaving campus when I saw him though."

Morgan wasn't interested in meeting the new boy, regardless of how attractive he may be. She was too busy pondering over what was causing the stone attacks and whether she had any avenues left to explore, places she hadn't yet thought of to look for information, to worry about such inconsequential things. From what she had seen so far, the petrification attacks hadn't affected anyone in the school yet, at least none that she had noticed. If only she could talk with the Mirror Man, she thought for the millionth time, he might have an idea on how to help her with the situation, just as he had helped her with the Cup of Jamshid.

She always thought better when she drew, so she opened her notebook to a blank page and began to sketch. Since her mind was on the petrification attacks, it was no surprise when the stone statue began to form on the page.

Hopefully the simple act of drawing would help her clear her mind and focus on class work.

Caught up in her own thoughts, she paid no attention when everyone settled into their seats, including the young man who walked through the noisy classroom to sit somewhere behind her and a couple rows over. She frowned her brows and added shading to the folds of clothing on the statue. Since this drawing was a statue, she looked over her selection of colored pencils and finally decided against all of them. There wasn't any reason to add color to stone. When the teacher started class a few minutes later, she tucked the page beneath her notebook, not entirely pleased with the way her drawing was turning out.

Her mind continued returning to her sketch throughout the class period. Instead of helping her to refocus and concentrate, it had brought about the opposite effect. She wondered whether other chosen throughout history had faced similar issues, not just in the balance between school and working for the fey but also in the depths of danger she and everyone around her now faced. There were about thirty students in her class, about the same in each of the other classrooms, bringing the school's population to well over a thousand, not counting the administrative staff who worked in the front office. While the petrification attacks in the human world seemed to be few and far between, Morgan knew better than to assume it would always stay that way. Whatever was turning the people to stone could easily impact everyone around her, herself included. What was worse was that unlike her, none of the people around her had any idea of the danger they were in.

She crumpled the statue and shoved the ball of paper into her backpack. While there was nothing she could do at that particular moment to help anyone in the school, she could at least pay attention so that if something came after them, she would notice.

When lunchtime rolled around, she followed Rebecca and Stacy to the cafeteria where the girls headed directly to a table that had obviously become their regular eating place. Despite the notes Liore had left in place for her, Morgan still knew next to nothing about the girls and remained quiet during the beginning of their conversation, hoping to avoid saying or doing anything that would seem out of place. Liore went to school in her place in order to keep Morgan's absences from being noticed but the more time Morgan spent in the fey world, the more of an outsider she felt in her own world. These were Liore's friends, not hers. This was Liore's daily routine, not hers. This was Liore's seat at the lunch table. None of it was Morgan's.

"May I join you?" A soft voice interrupted her thoughts and halted the conversation between Rebecca and Stacy.

Morgan looked up, mildly irritated at the interruption, wondering whether this was yet another thing she would need to keep track of. Her eyes fell on a young man of about the same age as herself, with snow-white hair and clear, vibrant sapphire eyes. She blinked once, twice, trying to clear the image from her eyes, certain that she was seeing things.

Rebecca immediately began to giggle, and Stacy scooted over to give the boy room to sit at their table. Morgan blinked in silence for a moment longer before shooting to her feet, almost knocking her chair over in the process. Her mouth slightly open in surprise, she looked from the boy to the pair of girls before her and back to him once more. "Come with me."

She stepped around the table, grabbed him by an arm, and practically dragged him out of the room. He barely had enough time to drop his backpack and lunch tray, so great was her hurry. She tugged him out of the cafeteria and down the hall, dragging him behind her as she went out the first exterior door she could find. When they were alone in the small atrium between the classrooms and the soccer field, she finally stopped and turned to face him. "What are you doing here?"

He smiled down at her, not bothered in the slightest by her reaction. "Attending school, just as you are." When she let go of his arm, he tugged the sleeve of his sweater back into place and adjusted the wristwatch so that it rested comfortably beneath the cuff.

"No, I mean what are you doing in this world? Everyone's been looking for you!" Her expression softened as she added, "I was worried about you."

"I am sorry." The smile faded as she spoke, and a small crease appeared between his brows. "I hadn't meant to worry you. With all of the attacks as of late, and the fact that the Ancients have been directly targeted, it was determined that I would be safest if I was closer to you."

"Closer to me?" she blinked in astonishment. "Why would you be safer closer to me?" As far as she could tell, he would have been far safer in his keep with the vicious bird guardian. "Things come after me all the time, wouldn't being here just put you in greater danger?"

"Perhaps. But you are also very aware of our world and able to see things that many others cannot."

"But..." she looked around. "Why can everyone see you? Shouldn't you be invisible? How can you attend school when you're fey?" Even as she asked, she knew the answer. If Liore could attend school and be visible to everyone, there must be some other mechanism involved, one that she was simply unaware of.

He shook his head. "I am visible because I am human. I am only considered an Ancient because of my incarnations."

Morgan slowly nodded her head, leaning back against one of the pillars that held up the overhang under which they stood. "I just... I wasn't expecting to see you here. I was worried about you and I was trying to figure out how to find you. Then suddenly you appeared. I thought I was going crazy for a minute there." Stormshock's reassurance that she would see him soon flowed through her mind. If only the dragon had been clearer on what he meant, she wouldn't have been so shocked to see him.

His gentle smile returned. "You are not crazy. I had wanted to warn you but there was little time. Then when I joined your class this morning, you appeared to be busy and I was seated elsewhere."

She blinked at him in surprise as she realized that the new student the girls in her class had been gossiping about had been him. Had she only been paying more attention instead of drawing the stone figure, she would have known of his presence hours ago. "So what are you called here? I can't imagine they're just calling you Mirror Man."

"Nathan Skett was the name I was given at

my most recent birth, so that is the name I am using now. Sometimes it comes in handy to be born a human."

Her mouth moved soundlessly as she processed the information. Although she had known that he was human, it had never occurred to her that he would have a human name. She had begun to get used to the strange names of the fey that his name just sounded... ordinary. The whole time she had known him, he had just been the Mirror Man, which was admittedly less of a name and more of a title. "Why didn't you tell me that was your name?"

His smile widened. "You did not ask."

Morgan's ears warmed as she realized he was right. Despite the amount of time she'd spent thinking about him, questioning his name had never been in her thoughts. "You said you know what's been going on with the petrification attacks? Do you know what's causing them, or how to help those who've been turned to stone?"

He shook his head sadly. "I have heard of them, that is true, but I have not yet found a solution to stopping the attacks or restoring those who have been afflicted." His eyes flashed as he added, "but I will continue my search and let you know as soon as I have more for you."

~ 7 ~

ANCIENT HISTORY

When they returned to the cafeteria, the animated whispering between Rebecca and Stacy halted as soon as Morgan and Nathan came into view. The girls watched their return with interest and no small amount of disappointment as they noticed Morgan was no longer holding his arm.

"Well?" Stacy demanded once both of them were seated. "Want to share the secret?" She raised one hand, palm up, invitingly.

"Yeah," Rebecca added. "What was that all about?" She looked between Morgan and Nathan with interest.

"I..." Morgan was getting tired of stammering. She swallowed hard and refused to look over at Nathan before answering. "I was just surprised, that's all. We actually already knew each other; I just hadn't realized he was transferring here." She didn't want to lie to the girls but she couldn't exactly tell them the truth, either. She just hoped that the explanation would be enough.

It was apparent that neither of the girls was completely fooled by her response but at least they didn't press for more information. Conversation quickly turned to safer topics, mostly involving the girls explaining some of the ins and outs of their school to Nathan. By the time lunch was over and they headed back to class, Morgan had begun to calm down.

Again, she and Nathan were in the same class, but this time she could see him from her desk. The first few times she had met him, she had reacted strongly to his presence, a reaction she still didn't understand. That reaction had been minimal during her interactions with him in the human world and she wondered whether that was due to a deliberate action on his part or if it was part of the world they currently inhabited. She also wondered whether others in the school were reacting to him as well, which could account for the heightened level of interest in him.

When class let out, Nathan was immediately accosted by a trio of girls. Morgan had hoped to speak with him more after school but that was apparently not to be the case. She swallowed her disappointment, slung her backpack over her shoulder and headed outside to see if her mother had remembered to come get her.

She had only walked about a block in the direction of her house before a familiar sensation washed over her. Her breath caught in her throat and she stumbled as her feet forgot how to move. The ground rushed up to meet her as her balance disappeared completely. A pair of steadying hands, one on her arm and the other on her opposite shoulder, kept her from tumbling to the ground. She looked up from the sidewalk to see a pair of concerned blue eyes surrounded by pale hair.

"Are you all right?" he asked as she regained her equilibrium. "Do you need to sit down?"

"No, I'm fine." Her mind slowly cleared as she steadied on her feet. Readjusting the strap of her backpack on her shoulder, she took a deep breath and willed herself to calm down. The feeling had been even stronger than it had the first time she had met him and she wasn't sure how much more of that she could handle. This time, she hadn't even seen him but she had known immediately that he was the cause. Apparently being in the human world hadn't dimmed his presence at all. "Really, I'll be okay."

"I am sorry, I hadn't meant to startle you like that." He released her arm and shoulder and stepped back, putting a blessed amount of distance between them. "I looked for you after class let out but you were already gone."

"It looked like you were talking with some of the other kids, so I didn't want to interrupt." She tilted her head and looked at him curiously. "Why didn't they react the same way I do to being around you? I mean, there are lots of people at the school but none of them seemed to really react all that much." At least, none that she had noticed. She had spent the morning too preoccupied with her own thoughts and the afternoon too busy thinking about him to have noticed much. People could have been dropping all over the place and she probably wouldn't have realized. She really needed to pay a lot more attention to what was going on around her.

"They had no reason to." He tilted his head to match hers. "I have no connection to others at the school, the only connection I have here is to you."

"I don't understand. I thought everyone around you would react like that."

Nathan chuckled softly. "No. Only those with whom I share a connection will react in any way to my presence. Some react more strongly and some react in different ways, depending on the type of connection we have, but people about whom I feel nothing feel nothing about me in return."

"People you feel..." she shook her head, refusing to believe what she had just heard. "But you were all alone!" She looked up at him with wide eyes. "You couldn't have connections to anyone being hidden away like that. Even the other fey, they all seemed to believe you were just some sort of a myth."

"I know." His smile faltered and he turned to walk in the direction of her house. "I am staying in this direction as well. I would like to accompany you, if I may."

Confused and uncertain, she nodded and stepped next to him. She didn't object to walking home with him but she wondered at the sudden shift in his demeanor. The sensation of his presence, almost overpowering only moments before, slowly faded as they walked. After two blocks, she looked sideways at his mask-like face. "Did I say something wrong?"

"You have said nothing wrong." He didn't turn to face her, which made her wonder how honest his response was. As though he sensed her question, he darted an eye sideways to look in her direction. "You are correct. I was alone for a very long time. You were the first person to visit me since I was placed in that fortress."

"Why were you placed there?" she asked. "I mean, I know that each of the Ancients has their own lair, their own place with guardians and such, but what happened to your parents?

Why don't you live with them? Even if you had to move there, why didn't they go with you?"

"They could have," he admitted. "In a few of my incarnations, my parents stayed with me until I was older. Most of the time, the people who give birth to me find my presence..." he looked away from her as he thought, "uncomfortable."

"What do you mean?"

"The connection between a parent and a child is a strong one. The reaction you feel when I am near you is nowhere near the response my families have all had to me. From the day I am born into any lifetime, they can feel it. Only a very few have been able to tolerate my presence for more than a handful of months."

"Months? You were brought there while you were still a baby?" When he nodded but didn't answer, she walked beside him for a few more steps, giving herself a moment to think. Her voice was much quieter when she finally spoke again. "How did you survive by yourself all that time?"

"At first, there were fey who stayed with me to care for me. It wasn't easy for them, as whenever I developed an attachment to any of them, they needed to be replaced. Eventually they began putting enchantments everywhere so that I could be cared for at a distance. For my last twenty or so incarnations, the only time I see anyone is when I am brought from the home of my parents to my home in the fortress. The enchantments there keep me alive and cared for until I am able to care for myself."

She wanted to ask more questions, to know more about the strange boy, but once he finished speaking, he appeared reluctant to explain further and she didn't want to press the issue. Before she knew it, they stopped at an intersection.

"I live down this way," he explained as he indicated the side street. "I enjoyed walking with you and I hope we can do it again."

Even though there had been very little conversation, she noted the absence of his presence immediately once he was gone. The aura that surrounded him did not return and a very small part of her missed it. As the sun peeked out from behind a pillow of clouds, she smiled at nothing in particular. She would see him again the next day and that would be enough.

"Finally home, I see." Liore lounged on Morgan's bed, immediately visible as soon as she stepped into her bedroom. "I thought you'd be home fifteen minutes ago."

"I was talking with a friend," Morgan explained as she settled her backpack next to her desk. "Am I being sent out again already?" While normally she would be excited at the prospect, the idea of leaving Nathan again so soon after having finally found him bothered her.

"Nope." When Morgan turned to look at her with one questioning eyebrow raised, the elvor grinned. "I'm actually here to start your magic lessons."

"Magic lessons?" She rushed to the girl's side, hoping she hadn't heard that wrong. "I'm finally gonna learn how to use magic?"

"Mhmm." Liore grinned at her excitement.

"But what about Corran? He specifically said that I wasn't supposed to learn any." Even though Magicgleam had said it was time for Morgan to be taught, she hadn't expected it to happen so soon. "Is he really okay with this?"

"Nope, but apparently he got overridden. Askel said that the orders came directly from Magicgleam so he didn't exactly have the option of saying no."

The grin that had threatened finally broke free. From the first time Morgan had seen Leander casting spells, she had been jealous of the former chosen who had been taught how to use magic as a part of his job with the fey. In fact, he had been taught by Corran himself, the same elvor who now refused to teach Morgan. It was unfair but at least the decision wasn't permanent. "So where do we start?"

They spent the rest of the evening learning about the language of magic, with a brief break only for dinner when the meal was ready. Morgan had seen the magical language a few times before, she even had a tome of spells she had uncovered on her journey but had been unable so far to read any of it. She had hoped that she would be able to cast some of the spells in the book, or even to identify what they were, but that was not to be the case.

"These are pretty high-level stuff," Liore

flipped through the pages of the book. "I'm surprised you still have this."

"Askel helped me the last time I needed to use a spell from there." She and the gryphon had teamed up to cast a spell to release a guardian who had been trapped under a pyramid. She still didn't understand how it had worked or why, but she was pleased that it had all turned out well in the end. She reached over and flipped a couple pages to show Liore the spell she had cast. "This is what we used to free the Ghirtablili."

"Heard about that," the elvor nodded slowly as she scanned the spell. "That's a good sign, though. We know that you are at least capable of casting a spell like this, so that gives us a good starting point."

Both of the fey moons were high overhead by the time they called it quits for the night, when Morgan couldn't focus enough to study any longer. Her eyes refused to follow the swirling lines on the page as she traced letter after letter, symbol after symbol, glyph after glyph, and her hands were cramping. She couldn't remember the last time she had written so much.

"It's a good thing you draw as much as you do," Liore commented as she packed up the small bag of supplies she had brought with her. "If you didn't, that would have been a lot harder."

Morgan had to agree. The years she had spent drawing and sketching everything she saw, or at least everything that caught her eye, helped her to trace the shapes of the strange alphabet and recreate them with only a few initial mistakes. There were still plenty more that she hadn't yet mastered but at least Liore was satisfied with the handful of symbols she had learned.

"Arien will be here tomorrow," she explained as she headed for the window. "He's going to teach you about some of the medicinal herbs and such in the area. He's also gonna teach you about what's safe to eat and what's not."

"Why is he coming here? Wouldn't it be better if I went out to see these things instead of everyone coming here?"

Liore shook her head. "The council decided that you haven't been able to spend enough time with humans lately, so they want to let you have as much of a normal life as you can while you're still able. This works out for me, too, as this means I get to go take that trip to the Biscayan Territories I've been wanting to go on for a while now."

"The Biscayan Territories?" Morgan knew of that area, she had been there a couple times recently. Not only had she made friends with a pair of druids who lived out in that area, Leander had gone to join them to learn how to become a druid in his own right.

"Yup, I'm going to visit Leander and a couple other friends I have out that way. But don't worry, I'll be back quickly if you end up needing me."

"We're not doing more magic tomorrow?" Much as she tried to keep the disappointment from her voice, even she could hear it clearly.

Liore laughed at that. "You think magic is just spellcasting?" She looked back over her shoulder at her one last time. "Don't let Arien hear you say that what he does isn't magic!" She stepped through the window and balanced on the narrow strip of roof that lay beyond.

"Besides, he knows more about the magical language than I do."

Morgan watched her friend disappear into the darkness, already missing her. It was nice to spend time with Liore again, they didn't get to spend much time together anymore. For the most part, the only time they sat and talked was when Morgan returned home after a period of time away. Even then, their time was spent hashing over what had been going on in the human world during her absence.

She was both pleased and nervous to see Arien. He had become a dear friend of hers while she had been working with the fey but she had reservations. While she had no reason whatsoever to mistrust him, she had doubts about almost all of the fey from Zea Island. She had her own reasons to believe that not everything was as it appeared and the conversations she had held with Stormshock and Magicgleam had only reinforced that opinion. There was simply too much going on, too much at stake, to take anything on pure faith alone.

~ 8 ~

MAGICAL TRAINING

"All of these can be used to create marks on trees or stone, ensuring you don't lose your way in a heavily forested area again." Arien's voice barely registered in Morgan's ears, but his next words pulled her from her reverie. "You do not appear to be paying much attention today. Is something amiss?"

"What?" Morgan blinked up at the apotharni in surprise. "No, everything's fine." She looked down at the pile of stones in her lap, trying to remember what the apotharni had told her each of them was. "Sorry, I guess I'm just a little distracted today."

"Yes, I can see that." Tucking his hooves beneath him, he settled down onto the grass next to her. As usual, the pair was slightly into the treeline at the edge of Morgan's back yard, almost completely hidden by the woods to any who happened to glance their way. They had spent the majority of the last three months in that spot, all the interaction Morgan had with the world of the fey had been reduced to her daily lessons with him. "It seems as though you have studied as much as you can for this day, so perhaps we should finish up for now." With one deft motion, he scooped the small pile of rocks from her lap and placed them back into his own satchel. "I haven't seen you with such a lack of focus in some time. Want to talk about it?"

Morgan leaned against his steady flank, feeling herself rise and fall slightly with his breathing. "I'm not really sure talking about it will help," she admitted finally. "It's a school thing, not exactly a fey thing."

Arien tilted his head in her direction. "Even if I cannot help directly," he looked down to meet her eyes, "sometimes just talking through what is bothering you can help to sort the issues in your mind. I have discovered that works well for me, as well as for many others. Just discussing the issue at hand does not always lead to a resolution but if it allows one to see the issue more clearly, that can open a path to move forward."

Morgan sighed and drooped her shoulders. He had a point, of course. He always did. She just wasn't sure how much she could or should tell him. There were things going on in the human world that directly impacted the world of the fey and she still wasn't sure how many of the fey she could trust. Much as she wanted to believe that Arien was among the trustworthy, she had believed the same of Corran until very recently. The knowledge that she had miscalculated so badly still stung and she was unwilling to put herself in the same position once more. "There's a new kid at school," she said finally. "He started only a little while ago, just after I got sent back here. He and I made friends pretty quickly but it's making some of the other kids in the class upset."

"Why are they upset because you and this new person are friends? It seems to me that everyone would want to be friendly, at least in the beginning."

She nodded. "True, and I think that's where the trouble is. It's a specific set of girls that are having a problem. You see, they're the popular girls and they don't think that Nathan should be friends with someone like me, they want him to be part of their group instead." The words she spoke were true enough. A girl named Brittany, one of the most popular girls in their grade and apparently one of the girls who had stopped Nathan after class on his first day, decided that she liked Nathan. When she realized that Morgan was friends with him, she began acting threateningly toward Morgan and her friends in an attempt to keep her away from him. Pretty shortly thereafter, more of Brittany's friends got involved as well, which only made a bad situation worse. While Morgan herself wasn't impressed by the childish threats made by Brittany and her friends, they were beginning to interfere with Morgan's own friends and her relationships with them. "If it was just me, I wouldn't really care. She's not really any sort of a threat to me but my other friends are really bothered by this. Bullying is a big problem and there isn't an easy way to stop it." Even if Rebecca and Stacy were more Liore's friends than Morgan's, she didn't want to damage their relationship.

"Is there nobody at your school to whom you can report these threats?" Arien asked. "If it is becoming this difficult for you and your friends, perhaps there is someone in a position to step in and assist with resolving this situation. A teacher or other adult?"

Morgan shook her head sadly. "Bad idea. Getting adults involved in things like this only makes them worse." Plus, she didn't want to risk calling any extra attention to the situation. Despite what she had told Arien, it wasn't just that Brittany and her friends didn't want Morgan to be friends with Nathan, Brittany was quickly becoming obsessed with the boy. If she didn't know better, Morgan would almost think that Nathan's aura had impacted her. Little did Brittany know that Nathan was no average boy and Morgan would do whatever she could in order to keep anyone from uncovering the truth about him. If he was hiding in the human world in order to stay safe, calling any attention to him at all was the last thing he needed.

The thought brought Morgan up short. Just what would happen if he was discovered? Would he have to leave and hide somewhere else? She hadn't known where he was while he was being moved from his fortress to the human world, so would she know where he was if he moved again? The gnawing sensation in the pit of her stomach returned in full force. She didn't want to lose him again; he had only been back for such a short time.

Although it was obvious that there was more than what she was telling him, Arien chose to remain silent on the matter for a few long moments after she stopped speaking before asking another question of his own. "Are you worried about your friends being harmed over this?"

Morgan considered the possibility. As much of a pain as the trio of popular girls were, she seriously doubted that they would do anything overtly to her friends because of the situation. After all, it wasn't like they had much choice in the matter. If anyone was to be targeted by them, it would be Morgan herself. "No," she said finally. "I'm pretty sure that they'll be fine no matter what happens."

"Does this boy mean that much to you, then?"

She looked up at the apotharni in surprise, feeling her mouth go dry at the question. Had he somehow figured out the truth? "I..." she stammered, "I don't really know. It's not like I've known him for all that long, of course, but I do like having him around." How could she explain without telling him everything? "More than anything, it annoys me when people like that think that they can control the people around them, just because they have something they want."

"Is there no possibility that this boy, this Nathan, could be friends with both you and these other girls?"

Morgan shook her head. "It's not like that, at least not exactly. She doesn't just want to be friends with him. She wants him to be her boy-friend, which would mean he wouldn't be able to be friends with me anymore. Or any other girls, really."

Arien tilted his head in confusion. "By being friends with a boy, that boy is no longer able to have other girls who are friends? Human inter-actions are so strange sometimes."

"It's more than just a friend thing. It's called a boyfriend, but it's more like a..." she tried to come up with a term that would make sense to the fey. "Like a lifemate, only not quite as seri-ous. Kinda like trying on a partner for a little while to see if you both make a good lifemate for each other."

"Ah, I see. A lesser romantic involvement, then. I have heard of such things." He looked up to the sky to gauge the height of the sun. "But I believe our time today has ended, as I believe you have human studies to complete as well. I will return tomorrow and we can pick up where we left off at that time." He pressed to his hooves and turned back to face Morgan. "I hope that you are better able to focus in the meantime."

"Me too," she said quietly as he disappeared into the trees.

Other than the issues with Brittany and her friends, there hadn't been very many issues in the human world that had required Morgan's attention. A handful of the fey had been to see Morgan, instructing her about the magical language and other similar things. Just as with Arien, she learned at home so the only interactions she had with the fey were when one showed up to tutor her. There hadn't even been many peri by to check on her, which was unusual. She had gotten used to the occasional presence of butterflies but lately there had been none. Even Tilson, loathe as he was to visit when he wasn't absolutely required, had been absent. Not for the first time, Morgan found herself wondering why the fey seemed to be keeping her at a distance.

Well, almost all of them. There was still one who frequently visited with her. Whether that was because he trusted her more than the other humans or simply because she was the only human he knew in her world, Morgan didn't know but it didn't matter.

To her great relief, she hadn't spotted any new statues lately, either human or fey. Without any real way of contacting Corran and the others on Zea Island, even if there had been more incidents of petrification, she wouldn't have been able to report them until someone came over to teach her. Still lost in thought, she picked up her notebook and pencil and made her way back into the house.

"You're not visiting with your friend today?" Susan, Morgan's mother, peered around the doorway to her office as Morgan walked past. "I figured you'd be long gone by now."

Morgan simply shook her head in response. "He has a bunch of homework left to catch up on and I need to study for a test tomorrow, so not today." Nathan had been a regular visitor to their house and Morgan's parents seemed to approve. Whether it was because they liked him as a person or whether they were simply happy that Morgan had finally started to make friends, she had no idea. Her parents, in turn, had no idea who Nathan truly was, for which Morgan was grateful. The last thing she needed was to answer any awkward questions.

In her room, she set the notebook and other supplies down onto her desk and sank onto the floor in front of her bed, crossing her arms on the mattress and settling her face into the space between. Closing her eyes, she did her best to clear her mind of all the random thoughts that fluttered through it, just as Liore had taught her. Without a clear head, she wouldn't be able to draw forth ether to use any of her own magic, a feat she found difficult enough to begin with. Although she had learned how to control small amounts of the ether, the magical energy that powered all of the fey and, to some degree, humans as well, she was still quite poor at it. With how little magical control she possessed, she wouldn't ever be able to perform even the simplest of spells, let alone any of the powerful spells in the book she possessed. To increase her ability, she trained in clearing her mind and drawing in the ether for at least fifteen minutes each day.

"Is now a bad time?" The calm, quiet voice pulled her out of her reverie.

"Not at all." She smiled over at the small mirror propped up on her desk. "I thought you were going to be busy today." As though the mirror had become a camera and monitor all in one, Nathan's face smiled at her through the glass. The first couple times he had used such a method for communication, it had surprised Morgan, but she had quickly become accustomed to seeing her own reflection re-placed by his. In the world of the fey, he was an Ancient called the Mirror Man, after all, so it only stood to reason that mirrors like the one they now used fell into his domain.

Nathan nodded. "I am, but I didn't get a chance to see much of you at all today and I wanted to see how you are doing."

As usual, his smile was equal parts shy and completely disarming, putting Morgan immedi-ately at ease. Even when he wasn't physically near her, just seeing him made her feel better, no matter how rough her day had been. "I'm doing okay. Arien came by for an herbalism lesson but we cut it short and he went back to the island a little while ago."

His smile faded and a small crease appeared between his brows. "Why was your training cut short?" Concern filled his eyes, darkening their color. "Herbalism is an important skill to have."

"I know," she sighed, "but I just couldn't concentrate today, that's all. We'll pick it up to-morrow when he comes by again."

"Do you need assistance? I can come over for a short while if that would help." He had been over to her house numerous times since coming to the human world. Often during his visits, he would teach Morgan tips and tricks to make her training go more smoothly, which had been the only reason she now understood the magical language. Without his help, she was certain she would still be struggling to decipher the cryptic symbols.

"No, that's okay," she said finally. Much as she wanted to see him in person, she didn't want to distract him too much from his own work, both as a student in school and as an Ancient. While she didn't fully understand what his job as an Ancient consisted of, it kept him busy enough for her to not question it.

The pair chatted amicably for a few moments before a rustling sound near the window drew Morgan's attention. The mirror through which they had been speaking immediately returned to its normal reflective state, with no indication that the Mirror Man had ever been. There was only one reason for him to disappear so quickly and so thoroughly, confirmed almost immediately by Tilson's fur-tipped tail peeking out from behind the curtains.

"Well, whaddaya know?" The haltija said irritably as he crawled up her leg to perch on the desk next to her. "You're actually awake this time."

"It's not even seven at night," Morgan responded absently. "Why would I be in bed this early?"

"How am I supposed to know why you do the things you do?" he demanded, tiny hands on his hips. "Why are you in bed at noon when I come to get you? Why are you still training in basic things like herbalism? Why don't you have your things ready to go already?"

"Go?" Morgan's eyebrows raised slightly. "Where am I going?"

Tilson sighed and tilted his head at her in annoyance. "Where are you going, she asks, as though she doesn't know why I would be sent here. Have you forgotten that we need you to do help us with problems too? Or are you so buried in your herbal training that you completely forgot about the rest of us?"

"Of course I hadn't forgotten about you guys," Morgan picked him up and settled him onto his usual spot on her shoulder, stood to her feet, and headed for the closet. Inside, her satchel, cloak, and staff waited, tools of her trade while working with the fey. No matter how little notice she had when she was called out, she took great care to ensure that her supplies were ready to go whenever someone came to fetch her. "What I don't know is where we are going or what's going on. The only fey I've seen lately has been Arien and he hadn't said anything about my being needed soon."

"Well of course Arien wouldn't have said anything," Tilson grumbled as he adjusted around the strap of her satchel. "He's your instructor, not your guide. That's what I'm here for. Now come on already, Askel is waiting outside."

Since it was obvious that getting any further information out of the haltija wasn't going to happen, Morgan simply looped the strap of her tree medallion around her neck and dropped the cloak over her shoulders. As silently as she possibly could, she snuck out of her bedroom, down the stairs, and out the back door. When she had first become a chosen, she had taken great care to keep her parents from noticing her absence but, after almost a year working with the fey, she had discovered that they had plenty of tricks to keep both her parents and her schoolmates fooled when she was gone. Sometimes an illusion was left in her place, usually when she took an overnight trip, but when she was gone for longer periods, Liore stood in for her. Morgan wasn't sure how long this particular trip would be, but she had faith that she wouldn't be missed in the meantime.

Except, she realized, by Nathan. There was no way the Ancient would be fooled by illusions or the guise of the elvor.

"Greetings, Morgan." Askel bowed his head low so that she could stroke his soft neck feathers. "You are ready to go?"

"Yes," she grunted as she climbed onto the gryphon's back. Although it had gotten easier to do so since the first time, she hadn't quite grown enough to make the process easy. "So what's going on this time?"

"Fey are disappearing," he explained as he trotted across the yard. "Seven have been lost so far: three were reported missing a few days ago and four who were sent to investigate have since disappeared as well. We dare not send more fey to investigate, so the council needs you to go find them and uncover what has happened to them."

"Do you think they're dead?" It was a distinct possibility as there had been more than just a few fey deaths since she had become chosen. However, given the recent circumstances, she doubted that it was anything so simple.

"Unlikely. We think they may have fallen victim to whatever had been causing the petrification a few months ago." He was quiet for a long moment before adding, "We have reason to believe that the human known as Bas-Grann may be behind the attacks somehow."

"Bas-Grann? What does he have to do with any of this?"

"Of that, I am uncertain," he admitted, "but the council recently met to discuss a request that he made to meet with the High Council. His missive indicated that if they refused his demand for a meeting, he would do something drastic, so much so that he could not be ignored by either fey or humans."

"And you think that a handful of missing fey are what he was talking about?" Morgan wasn't so sure about that idea. While she was hardly in favor of having anyone – human or fey – disappear, she couldn't help but question it. "Sounds a little tame to be considered that drastic, if you ask me."

~ 9 ~

LABYRINTH

Sad to have to leave Nathan behind yet again and thoughtful about Bas-Grann's latest demand, Morgan was quiet for most of the ride. She couldn't fathom what the magus was up to now, or what the missing fey had to do with the big plan he had threatened. While she could understand the concern from the fey, as losing any of their own was a bad thing, she didn't see how it would draw the attention of the humans. It simply didn't add up. The trip wasn't nearly as long as the trips they normally took were, so she was surprised when Askel circled to land before the sun had fully settled below the horizon. "Are we here already?"

"Yes we are," he answered as he trotted to a stop. "This was the last place they were reported to be."

They were on a small island, covered with rocky outcroppings and dotted with scrub trees and a few bushes but little else to be found. As far as she could tell, there was nothing of interest to the fey on the island that would have drawn those who disappeared there. "What on earth were they doing here?"

"I have no answers for that."

She slid to the ground, discovering that the stones were solid but slippery. After taking a moment to regain her balance, she stepped away from the gryphon and began to explore.

"Hey, wait for me!" Tilson's shrill voice called from behind her. He had dropped to the ground as well but did not manage to maintain his footing. As he wobbled to his feet, Morgan reached down to scoop him up and tuck him securely into her hood. "I can't believe you were just going to leave me behind," he grumbled as he brushed damp moss from his fur. "After everything I've done for you, too. I'd expect you to be just a little more grateful."

Ignoring his complaints, Morgan climbed onto one of the rocky formations to get a better view of the island. The mass that she had originally believed to be quite small turned out to be much larger than her initial view had led her to believe, as the island extended a distance beyond the rocks, jutting far into the surrounding ocean. "Let's take a look over there." She didn't immediately see anything that drew her attention, but it was the only place available to investigate.

"I shall wait here," Askel called after them. "My claws aren't as sturdy on these types of ground as yours are."

Morgan waved at him as she climbed down the other side of the rocks. "We shouldn't be too long," she called over her shoulder. "There isn't a lot here to explore, after all." Just as she finished speaking, the ground beneath her fell away and she found herself half-sliding, half-falling through a narrow tunnel. The edges were blessedly smooth, which kept her from snagging on the walls as she fell. Tilson's shrieks matched her own, echoing off the narrow confines as they descended deeper underground.

After only a few seconds, they hit the bottom of the tunnel with a thump. The angle of descent kept her from being seriously injured in the fall but as Morgan regained her footing on the slick stone floor, she evaluated the path from which they had come. "There's no way I'm getting back up that way," she said, mostly to herself.

Tilson, finally realizing that they had stopped falling, took a shuddering breath and looked up as well, where a tiny patch of sky showed how far they had fallen. "I don't think I can climb that either," he agreed. "Why weren't you paying more attention to where you stepped?"

A shadow fell over the entrance high above and Askel's voice called down to them. "Morgan? Tilson? Are you both all right?"

"Yeah," Morgan called up to him. "We're fine but we're not gonna be able to get back out that way."

"I will notify the council of what has happened. There was no knowledge of a subterranean area on this island."

"No kidding," Morgan sighed, her voice not loud enough to reach her friend above. Raising her voice again, she called up, "We're going to see if there's another way out of here. But I think we found what happened to the fey who went missing."

"Do you see any signs of them down there?"

"Not yet but it looks like the area down here is a bit bigger than I thought, so we can check it out. Hopefully there's an exit somewhere, too."

"Good thing I have a flashlight," Tilson offered as he switched on his tiny light. "It's not much but better than the dark would be."

Morgan nodded and rummaged around in her own satchel, searching for her own flashlight. When she finally located it, pulled it free, and turned it on to shine around the area, she let out a low whistle. "This place is huge."

Tilson nodded, his whiskers brushing lightly against her neck. "And there's more than one tunnel, too. See?" He pointed his light in a different direction from where Morgan had been looking, revealing a fork in the tunnel. "We're never going to find our way out of here."

"Maybe," Morgan answered absently. As her

light played across the tunnel system, she noticed an assortment of stones that had tumbled down from above. "But maybe not. Look!" She rushed forward to pick up a familiar-looking stone. "This is one of the rocks Arien taught me about."

Tilson looked at the pebble doubtfully. "What good is a rock going to do us? Will it help us get out of here?"

"Not on its own, no. But it does this." She reached out and used the rock to draw a mark on the wall. "We can use marks like this to know where we've been so we don't get lost." Although she hadn't been paying much attention while Arien had taught her all of the properties of the rock she now held, she had paid enough just enough attention to remember that druids often used rocks similar to the one she had found to mark paths through unfamiliar forests. She added a second mark and then a third to her initial drawing, creating an arrow. "Now we know which way we've already gone, so if we end up back here again, we'll know which way we haven't explored yet."

Overruling the haltija's protests that they

should just stay put and wait for help, Morgan headed in the direction she had drawn the arrow, seeking a way out of the cave. Only a few steps further, she stopped and held a hand up to shush her friend. "Did you hear that?"

"Hear what?"

"I thought I heard something up ahead." She strained to listen but the fleeting noise she had heard was gone. "Maybe it was just an echo," she decided finally. Shrugging, more to herself than for any other reason, she hitched her satchel more securely onto her shoulder and continued down the dark tunnel, occasionally marking the walls as she passed. A few more times she stopped to listen, sure that she had heard the distant noises again, but every time she tried to hear the sounds more clearly, they were gone.

They passed tunnels that led off to the right and left, some veering in the same direction as the one they were headed and others curving back in the direction from which they had come. Each time they encountered a side passage, Morgan stopped to examine the opening, listening for more of the fleeting sounds that she was becoming less and less convinced were echoes, before marking the wall to indicate the direction they traveled and continuing. Twice, she reached a dead-end where the tunnel she chose could continue no further. Each time, she backtracked to the most recent offshoot, marked the walls to show that there was an end to the tunnel they had been on and to show in which new direction she had chosen. Five times she repeated the process before arriving at a tunnel with a familiar mark on it.

"We're traveling in circles!" Tilson proclaimed as he pointed his light at the arrow scratched into the wall.

"Yeah," Morgan agreed. "This place is like a big, underground maze." She sighed and examined her options.

"I guess that's why the fey have been disappearing from here," Tilson sighed. "If any of them fell down into this place, there's no way they'd make their way back out."

Morgan had to agree. Unless the fey who had disappeared were able to fly like the peri, she couldn't imagine how any of them would be able to escape the underground tunnels, particularly if they didn't have a way to see in the dark.

"Wait a second." Tilson balanced on her shoulder, holding her hair for support and leaning forward, shining his light ahead into the blackness before them. "I just heard something."

"Yeah, I know. That's the same thing I've been hearing the whole time." She nudged him back more securely onto her shoulder so that he didn't tug at her hair so much. "I still can't tell what it is, though."

"Maybe it's the missing fey," he suggested. "Maybe they really did get trapped down here."

"Kinda what I was wondering, too." She didn't want to admit that she had been secretly hoping that was all it was. If the noise was caused by the fey who had gone missing from the tiny island, their job was complete once they rescued them and brough them back to the surface. However, her mind kept returning to the Djieien, the massive spider Ancient who had attacked her recently. The closest it had come to killing her had been in her own backyard, where it had dug a tunnel underground which she had fallen into. At the time, she had been a little too busy just trying to survive the encounter to examine the hole the creature had trapped her inside but now she had to wonder if these tunnels had been made by a similar creature.

Oblivious to her inner thoughts, Tilson continued chattering. "We should try calling out to them," he suggested. "They might not even know that we're here looking for them."

"We could do that," she agreed, "but what if we're wrong and it's not the fey making those noises? We could end up putting ourselves into danger by calling out and letting whoever lives down here know that we're in their house."

The noises continued even as they discussed, no longer fleeting sounds that could have been figments of their imaginations. They soon reverberated from the cavern walls and Morgan wracked her brain trying to figure out what the sounds could mean.

"I think you're right," Tilson said, much more quietly than before. "That doesn't sound like any of the fey I know."

"Yeah," she answered equally quietly. "That's

what I was thinking too." The sounds turned into scraping, scratching noises that thundered in a regular pattern.

THUD ... *skeeeet* ... THUD ... *skeeeet* ... THUD

"Whatever that is, I don't think I like it." The haltija switched off his tiny light and slipped from Morgan's shoulder and into the hood of her sweater. "Maybe we should move a little faster." If there was one thing certain to keep the haltija quiet, it was the threat of potential danger. Even the idea that he could be in peril was usually enough to make him run for cover.

...skeeeet...

"But where?" Morgan asked, her voice barely audible. "I can't even tell where those sounds are coming from!"

THUD

They crept along the passage, continuing in the same direction they had been heading. Morgan remained as quiet as she could be, straining her ears to figure out whether the sounds were getting louder because she was headed toward whatever was causing them or whether it was because whatever was causing them was getting closer to her. No matter how she turned her head, how she cocked her ears at every intersection, the sound seemed to be coming from every direction she looked.

...skeeeet...

As she crept into yet another of the seemingly endless tunnels, absently marking the wall as she went, another sound joined the echoing noises. This one sounded more like heavy thumps of metal rattling against metal. "No way," she breathed. "There's no way he'd be all the way down here."

"He who?" Tilson asked over her shoulder. "Do you know who's making that sound?"

"I sure hope not." As they crept further down the tunnel, the pursuing noises seemed to fade but the clanking sounds increased in volume. Relief flowed through her that at least one of the mysterious sounds seemed to be less of a threat, she paused for a moment in the tunnel to gather her thoughts and take a breath that wasn't tainted by the flavor of fear.

"Who do you think is up there?" Tilson asked. "And why did you stop?"

"I just needed a second," she responded. "At first, I thought the sounds ahead seemed kind of like the sounds we heard back when we took the hammer from Volcan."

"Volcan?!" Tilson squealed, covering his mouth with his tiny hands. "You think Volcan is down here?"

She shook her head. "No, I don't think so. I think it just sounds similar but it's not the same noises."

"Good thing," he breathed. "You really scared me with that one."

"Me too." She hitched her satchel onto her shoulder again and headed down the tunnel once more. "I think the last thing we need is to run into him again. Besides, I think these tunnels are a bit too small for him."

As they approached the source of the second set of noises, Morgan covered her light with one of her hands. Barely any light escaped her grasp but in the inky blackness that surrounded them, it was plenty to navigate by. Soon, she spotted a dim light from further ahead and she crept warily toward it, turning off her flashlight completely once the tunnel was illuminated enough for her to be able to navigate.

The tunnel opened into a massive room with

row upon row of iron cages hanging from hooks on the ceiling. "This is kinda like the cage we were in when we got caught by the pygmies," Tilson whispered in her ear, "except these aren't made of branches and stuff."

"Mhmm," she nodded as she examined the closest cage. Rust and grime covered the base but it was clearly evident that nothing was hidden inside. The clanking sounds that had drawn them into the room sounded much closer than they had while she and Tilson had been in the tunnel so she followed the sound.

A few rows further into the room, they discovered that not all of the cages were empty. Some had what appeared to be piles of filthy rags and broken, bleached-white sticks in them but others held assorted weaponry and clothes. One even had what seemed to be an old helmet, but Morgan didn't want to get close enough to find out for certain. The last thing she wanted to discover at that moment was whether or not the helmet was empty.

It didn't take very long to find the source of the noise. One cage swung slightly from side to side, the hook on the ceiling grating against the cage suspended below it. As the metal rubbed against metal, it created the clanking noise she had heard. A pair of dvergar huddled in the cage, neither of which seemed to be much older than Morgan herself.

"Hey," she called up quietly to the pair. "Are you guys okay?"

Startled, the dvergar jerked and whimpered as they looked around the area. Finally they noticed the girl standing a few feet away, at which time they calmed considerably. "What are you doing here?" one of them asked. "You will be captured too."

"Where are the others?" None of the other cages appeared to hold the rest of the missing fey.

"They were already taken," one of them offered.

"Eaten, most likely. Leave while you still can," the other agreed. "You do not want to be here when he gets back."

"When who gets back?"

The dvergar gasped and backed away from her, their eyes locked on something deeper in the cavern. Following their gaze, Morgan spotted a massive creature headed in their direction. "Centaur," the word caught in her throat.

"Not a centaur," Tilson disagreed. "There's only two legs."

The single pair of legs weren't the only thing that differentiated the massive creature from the centaur she had initially believed it to be. Atop its head grew a pair of massive horns, each of which was longer than Morgan's arm.

"What do you think you are doing, intruder?" The newcomer's voice reverberated from the cavern walls, thundering into Morgan's ears. "This area belongs to me alone. Any who enter my domain are forfeit."

Backing away from the massive creature, Morgan's eyes swept back and forth, seeking anything that could help the situation. An assortment of broken weapons and more heaps of cloth were littered everywhere but none of them seemed to be of any use. At least, she thought, they probably hadn't been all that useful to whoever brought them down here.

The cage holding the dvergar squeaked again as the pair of captives backed away from their captor. "Do you think you can unlock that cage?" Morgan whispered to Tilson, trying to maintain her distance from the menacing creature.

"Probably," he whispered back. "Wait, you don't expect to leave me here, do you?"

"I'm not going to leave you," she reassured him, "but we need to get them to safety."

"And where's safety?"

"Back where we came in. Just follow the marks on the wall."

"But that's not safe, we couldn't get out that way. That's how we got here in the first place, looking for a way out!"

"I know. But Askel should be back with help by now." She stumbled but refused to look down at whatever she had tripped over, not wanting to see what could have been smooth and rounded in a heap of cloth on the floor. "Just get them there. I'll be right behind you."

"What're you going to do?"

"Someone has to get that thing away from here so you guys can escape." She paused with her shoulder against one of the cages, waiting for the haltija to climb off. "You're small enough to get across to them and get them out. I'm not.

But if I can get him to chase me, that should give you enough time to release them and get them out of here."

Despite his continuing protests, she changed direction as soon as she felt his weight lift from her shoulder. Praying that the creature hadn't realized she wasn't alone, she moved away from where Tilson hid behind a cage bar.

There were multiple exits from the chamber, not just the one through which she and Tilson had entered and the one that was still blocked by the prison-keeper. All she needed was enough space between herself and the creature she believed to be a minotaur. On one hand, she wondered whether it was called something different than what she had understood it to be called, as many of the fey had names different than those known to humans but on the other hand, she didn't care. It wasn't like she was going to be horribly bothered if she offended it by using the wrong term.

"Hey, ugly!" She stepped into full view of the minotaur and faced it directly. Thankfully it wasn't carrying any weapons and she briefly wondered whether it had been the cause of the booming and scraping noises she had heard earlier. Whether he had been or not, she needed to chance it. "You want me, you gotta come get me!"

With his full attention on her, she darted to the edge of the cavern, headed for the closest exit. The beast bellowed as it gave chase, its substantial hooves clattering across the floor and scattering heaps of debris as it followed her into the darkness. She hoped that it was as blinded by the lightless cavern system as she herself was but had little faith in such. There was no reason for anything to live in darkness unless that was where it was comfortable. She kept one hand on the wall of the cavern as she ran, scraping fingertips against rough stone, searching for the offshoot that she knew had to be there somewhere.

When the wall disappeared from her hand, she changed direction, slamming into the wall on the far side of her new tunnel in her haste to make the turn. The minotaur wasn't far behind, as the ever-approaching sound of his hooves attested, so she didn't bother trying to catch her balance. She dropped to the ground, pulled her cloak as tightly around herself as she could, and skittered to the opposite side of the tunnel where she huddled in silence, pressed as tightly against the wall as she could, holding her breath and praying that her plan would succeed.

While she was at it, she hoped that the minotaur would take the corner as widely as she herself had and wouldn't accidentally trample her as he moved.

Hooves and rank odor flew past her as she squeezed her eyes shut, more in reflex than in any belief that it would help. As the sounds continued down the passage, she risked cracking an eye to glance around, knowing full well that she wouldn't see anything even if the minotaur was directly in front of her. The echoes of clacking hooves continued in the distance as she crept as silently and carefully as possible back down the tunnel toward the main chamber.

Where she had thought she had only run a short distance before finding the offshoot passage that had become her hiding place, she discovered on the return trip that she had moved a lot further away from Tilson and the dvergar than she had expected. She just hoped she had put enough distance between them and the minotaur for them to reach safety.

In the main chamber, the dozens of cages still waited in silence for their next victims. The cage that had held the dvergar was empty and Morgan let out a sigh of relief as she realized that her plan had worked. By now, she figured, they had to be halfway back to the opening where she and Tilson had fallen into the labyrinth.

Keeping her cloak tightly closed around her and moving slowly enough to remain invisible to the massive creature in case it returned, Morgan followed the markings she had placed on the walls, the same markings she hoped had led the others to safety. She knew the very moment that the minotaur realized her deception as his bellow of rage crashed over her, echoing off of the walls and causing small pebbles across the floor to rattle. She stopped and let out an unintentional gasp of surprise when she heard the sound, uncertain as to how far away the creature was.

Although she knew that the arrows she had drawn along the walls would eventually lead back to the entrance, she had crisscrossed her own path a few times in her initial exploration of the cave system and had to double-back more than once as she followed her markings to one dead-end after another. It appeared she hadn't been quite as thorough at marking the dead-end passages as she had intended while exploring the caves. When she spotted the dim light in the distance, she was sure she was only imagining it but as she approached the source of the light, she saw shadowed forms on the ground in a rough circle of bright light.

"She's here!" Tilson squealed. "I told you she'd make it!"

"Indeed," Askel agreed. "Now let's get her up and out of there so we can all be rid of this place."

A rough rope had been lowered into the hole, with knots tied every foot or so along its length. The knots made climbing much easier, which Morgan greatly appreciated as she made her ascent. When her head crested the surface, she noticed that Glau was there as well, which explained how the rescued dvergar would be able to leave with them.

"Are you alright?" Askel asked as soon as Morgan was back on the surface.

"Yeah," Morgan nodded. "Just glad to be out of there. Can we go home now?"

"Absolutely."

~ 10 ~

RELEASE AND RETREAT

Morgan slept fitfully on the trip back to Zea Island. Her dreams were filled with shadowy caverns, stone statues of people she knew, and massive spiders that chased her from scene to scene. She woke with a start as the sun was cresting over the horizon, jerking enough that Askel had to adjust his flight pattern to keep from dropping her.

"Are you all right?" he called to her between his beating wings.

"Yeah." She groaned and stretched, looking

around to figure out how much further they needed to travel. "Just a bad dream."

"With everything that has been going on lately, I would be surprised if you were not having trouble sleeping."

"Why you having sleep problems?" Tilson grumbled irritably. "I've been sleeping just fine, until someone almost kicked me out into the clouds."

"Sorry about that," Morgan responded absently. "How much further do we have to go? I think I recognize a few of those mountains over there." The small range of mountains in the distance looked familiar, as though they had flown past them on more than one occasion.

"As you should by now. Those mountains mean that we are almost home."

"Thought so." She dug through her bag to grab a granola bar, which had become her go-to breakfast while out with the fey. At first, she had been pleased to have granola bars all the time but had quickly gotten bored with them. The variety of bars available at her local grocery store kept her from finding something to replace them with, however, so as long as she could change up the flavor every now and again, it was worth it. Plus, even when one of them got smashed in her bag, it tasted exactly the same as it would have otherwise.

Just under two hours later, they came to land in the clearing in the center of Zea Island. As usual, many of the fey gathered to greet them. "Welcome back," Arien stepped forward to help her to the ground. "We are all pleased to see your safe return."

Once she had her footing, Morgan looked around the clearing and then back up at the sky. "Where did Glau go?" She turned her attention back to the gryphon.

"He took the dvergar home."

"Oh." Morgan was a little disappointed that she wouldn't get the opportunity to speak with either Glau, with whom she had recently formed a friendship, or to meet the dvergar she had helped to rescue.

"Please," Corran stepped through the gathered fey. "Let her have some room. We are all eager to hear of what happened but she has only just arrived."

Despite her suspicions about the elvor,

Morgan was still pleased to see him. Corran had been one of the first fey she had met and even though his demeanor was often stand-offish at best, she liked him. She just wished that she could trust him again like she used to. "No, really, I'm okay. Everything's fine now and we're both safe." She caught the haltija as he jumped from Askel's back to land on her shoulder. "See? Both of us are just fine."

"We are all eager to hear about your findings," Corran said as he led her to the edge of the clearing. "Askel of course told us of your misadventure after you fell into the ground but none of us knows what befell you after that."

"Misadventure. That's a good word for it. Actually, that reminds me. There is a creature I know of called a minotaur, part bull and part human. Do you know of a creature like that?"

"We do. We also call such creatures mino-taurs."

"Interesting." She hadn't expected that. Almost every creature she had met was called something else by the fey, so it was a surprise that they shared their name across the veil. "Did you guys know there was one on that island?"

Corran's eyes widened and he took a step back in obvious surprise. "A minotaur? Are you certain of this?" His golden skin even seemed to lose a shade of color at the question. A gasp rippled through the fey who had followed them to the treeline.

Morgan nodded. "That's what caught the dvergar. They were in this big room full of cages."

"I rescued them!" Tilson hopped to a branch of the nearest tree and stood as tall as his six inches of height would allow. "That was all me."

Morgan nodded her agreement. "When we found the dvergar, we didn't know that there was a minotaur there. We knew there was something, but not what it was. Then this huge thing came charging into the room and we had to run from it." She described how Tilson had released the dvergar from their prison while she had diverted the minotaur.

"But how did you escape? Those creatures, as I understand, are quite swift."

She nodded emphatically. "That one sure was fast. For a minute there, I wasn't sure I was going to get away from it. But my cloak saved me." She explained how she had hidden and used the cloak to conceal herself while the creature ran past her into the tunnels beyond. "Thankfully, by the time we all got back to the opening, Askel was back with that rope to get us out."

"Minotaurs have not been seen for a great many years," Arien supplied. "That is why we are all highly surprised that you encountered one of them."

Corran nodded his agreement. "The very first high council, now referred to as the First Council, locked away all of the minotaurs years ago. They were deemed too dangerous to leave free, so they were never supposed to be released. For you to encounter one means that something has gone horribly wrong."

"You mean they missed one?" Morgan hoped that was the case. "I mean, that would make sense. If one of them managed to stay hidden for that long, that underground maze was going to be a good place to stay out of sight." She accepted the cup of sweet-smelling tea that Arien offered her, not even questioning what was in it. After a swallow or two, she took a deep breath and finally felt herself start to relax. "Or are you thinking that one of them that was captured managed to escape?"

"I am uncertain as to what this means," Corran admitted. "But I will have to notify the other councils of what you have discovered."

Morgan watched him walk away, many of the fey following him as he left. Once everyone was out of earshot, she turned back to Arien. "Why did the First Council lock the minotaurs away? I understand they're pretty dangerous but that doesn't really explain why they were all taken. I mean, centaurs are pretty dangerous too, but nobody locked them all up, did they?" She couldn't quite wrap her mind around the logic of locking away an entire race. If some of them misbehaved, why had all of them paid the price?

"You are correct, the centaurs were not locked away as the minotaurs were. In fact, there were only a handful of species who were treated in such a manner. But there was a very good reason why it happened in the first time."

Morgan looked up at him expectantly as she took another sip of the tea. Where Corran hesitated to tell her anything about anything, Arien always knew the history of things, so she wasn't surprised that he had a story about the minotaur as well. She pressed her back against the trunk of the same tree Tilson was still in and slid down the rough bark of its trunk to sit and listen.

"Some of the fey races," Arien began as he settled to the ground as well, tucking his hooves beneath him, "didn't like that the First Council was willing to work with humans. They tried to stage a revolt, believing that the fey did not need to involve themselves with anything in the human world. It was an ugly fight, one that did not end quickly, but those who opposed the maintenance of our relationship with humans were defeated. Those who refused to cooperate with the First Council's decision were locked away for fear that they would attempt to revolt again, should the opportunity arise once more."

"Like the minotaurs." It wasn't a question, as she already understood the answer.

"Among others. But the minotaurs were among them, yes."

"Was it all of the minotaurs or just some of them?"

"As I understand, all of them decided to oppose the decision."

"What about the other races, those who originally objected but changed their minds and decided to cooperate?" Morgan asked. "They weren't locked away too, were they?"

"No," Arien agreed, "they were not. All who were allowed to maintain their freedom have been heavily monitored since that time, however, to ensure that they continue to follow the laws of the Council."

"Do you think it was one of them who released the minotaur?"

"It is possible, but that line of thought leads to a much larger and more important question."

Morgan furrowed her brows as she tried to follow the apotharni's train of logic. "What question?"

"If the minotaur was released, which appears to be the most logical answer, then the question becomes were there others that were released as well? I find it difficult to believe that anyone, fey or human, would go through the trouble of freeing the minotaur and only release one. That means there are likely more of them out there somewhere. And if there are minotaurs out and about again, there are likely others besides just the minotaurs who were let out to roam freely."

Morgan nodded slowly as the realization dawned. "There's not really a whole lot more effort in releasing lots of fey than there would be in releasing just one. And if someone really did want to start that revolt you mentioned again, then letting out just one single minotaur wouldn't really do much."

"Your logic is sound. That is the same conclusion to which I also arrived." Deep in their conversation as Morgan and Arien were, neither noticed as Corran joined them until the elvor spoke. "I have already sent word to the other councils to report what you have found and to request that they let us know if anything further about these dangerous fey is discovered."

"So we just wait?"

"That appears to be the most reasonable course for us at this moment," he agreed. "Without further information upon which we can act, there is little more for us to do."

"What's going on over there?" Arien directed the group's attention to a small gathering of fey. A handful of them, many of whom Morgan had seen often on the island, appeared to be carrying packs of equipment to the center of the clearing.

Corran sighed. "The dvergar," he explained. "They have been ordered to retreat from the council. Not just from ours, from all of them. They are all being called back to their homeland."

Morgan was even more confused at his statement than she had been during the entire conversation with Arien. "Ordered to retreat? By who? Don't all of the fey here answer to the council?"

"No," the elvor shook his head slowly. "Not all of the fey here answer only to the council. Just as with the tribe of cats who work with us but who ultimately answer to their king, the dvergar have a similar structure. These dvergar were assigned to us but they ultimately answer to their chieftain, Alberich."

She hadn't heard that name before. "Who is Alberich?"

"Remember how the cats have their king?" Finally deciding to rejoin the conversation, Tilson dropped onto her lap. "Alberich is kind of like their king. And the dvergar we have here were kind of like Tekli, in that they answer to their king but he lets them work with us."

"And their chieftain, this Alberich, he doesn't want them working with us anymore?"

"I had feared something like this may happen," Corran said. "The release of the minotaur was only the most recent indicator that someone is attempting to shift the balance of power. Our meetings with Alberich had already been strained before this latest event. He had been hinting for some time that the dvergar may withdraw if it appears things will become too dangerous for them. It appears that decision has been made."

Morgan watched, appalled, as the handful of dvergar finished gathering their belongings and said their goodbyes. "I don't understand," she whispered. "Everyone was dying not long ago but that wasn't dangerous enough to call them home. Why now? What changed?"

"Everything." Corran didn't bother to look at

her as he spoke. "If the convicted fey are being released, that changes everything."

~ 11 ~

CLOSE TO HOME

As had long since become her habit, Morgan settled down to sleep under a tree at the edge of the clearing. The first few times she had slept on the island had been odd, wondering whether she would wake up to discover it had all become a dream. Over the time she had spent among the fey, however, her time in in the human world had become more like the dream world to the fey's reality. Much as she loved her bed, with its mounds of soft pillows and warm blankets, she also loved the feel of the breeze on her face as she slept and the sight of the clouds and stars drifting slowly by as she settled down for the night and the welcoming beams of the sun's first rays when she woke. Even when she was home, safe in her own bed, she had taken to sleeping with the window open, both to allow the breeze in and to allow the fey to come visit when they wanted.

She yawned and stretched, wondering when she had covered herself in her Cloak of Concealment. She knew that she had worn the cloak on the ride to the island the previous night, but she could have sworn she had tucked it into her satchel, as she hardly needed concealment on the island and the weather was still warm enough to not need the cover. She rubbed at her eyes to clear the sleep and looked around, surprised to find that Tilson wasn't curled up in his usual position next to her. As her vision focused on the figures in the clearing, she froze, certain she was still asleep and this was just a very strange, very bad dream.

As always, the assorted fey were everywhere across the clearing. Some were settled underneath trees to rest as she herself was but most appeared to be milling about across the clearing, tending to one task or another. Everything she spotted seemed to be perfectly normal at first glance, except for the fact that not a single one of the figures in the clearing moved. No sounds flowed through the clearing, none of the low-lying chatter to which she had become accustomed. Only the distant sound of birds could be detected.

"They're all frozen," she whispered to herself in horror, "oh no!" Not far from her sleeping position, she spotted Arien, hooves tucked beneath his form, head lowered as though in rest. She scrambled to his side, hoping to find him merely sleeping but before she reached him, she knew the truth. His skin and fur were smooth and cold to the touch. "No, no, no...." she whimpered as she ran her fingertips over what remained of her friend.

She bolted to her feet, her breath catching in her throat and her pulse thundering in her ears, and ran around the clearing, checking on all of the fey to see if any remained alive. She found peri statues tucked into the branches of a tree, elvor who appeared to have been deep in conversation when they became petrified, and plenty of others. Corran was nowhere to be seen, nor were Askel or Tilson. Just to be sure, Morgan checked all of the statues once more, searching for the haltija. Part of her needed desperately to find her friend but a much larger prayed that she wouldn't find him. To her relief, Tilson was nowhere to be found.

"Tilson?" She cupped her hands around her mouth to amplify the sound and called for him. "Askel? Corran? Anyone?" Back and forth across the clearing she walked, calling for each of them in turn.

"What is the meaning of all this shouting?" Corran demanded as he walked calmly into view. "I could practically hear you from the other side of the river."

"Corran!" Morgan cried out in relief. "You're okay!"

"Of course I'm okay." He peeled the girl away from him and looked down at her in confusion. "What has you so worked up so suddenly?"

"They're all gone," she sobbed. "Arien, everyone. They've all been turned to stone."

The expression of impatient confusion that had taken up residence on Corran's face was replaced by the raised eyebrows and slack jaw of shock at her words. He stepped around Morgan and surveyed the area, his eyes dancing from one statue to the next. "When did this happen?" he demanded. "And who is responsible?"

"I don't know," she answered. "They were all like this when I woke up." She explained how she had discovered them after waking beneath her cloak. "Someone had to have put it over me," she explained. "Otherwise I'd be a statue right now too."

"Lucky you were for that," Corran answered, the sharp edge of his voice gone completely. "Else we could have lost you as well. Tell me, did you see anything last night? Any indication of what caused this?" When she shook her head in response, still wiping away tears, he pressed for more information. "Do you have any idea who placed your cloak over you?"

"I don't know," she answered finally. "At first, I thought maybe it could have been Tilson, he has a habit of going through my things while I'm sleeping, but my cloak is pretty big and it would have been hard for him to manage. Then I thought maybe it was Arien. He's usually watching out over me." It wouldn't have been the first time she had gone to sleep uncovered and woken to find a blanket or such over her.

"Yes, that would make sense," Corran agreed. "He has always felt quite protective over you, over all of the chosen. But I am not sure that he is responsible for your safety this time."

"Yeah, I don't think so either. If he'd seen someone coming to attack, someone dangerous enough for him to cover me up like that, he wouldn't have just gone back to sleep like that."

"Precisely. But regardless of who is responsible for your salvation, you need to be relocated immediately. It is obviously not safe for you here, so I believe it is best for you to go home. I will send for Tekli to accompany you and to watch over you once you are back in your world."

Morgan couldn't disagree with his assessment. They had been attacked while she slept, so safety was not a word she could associate with Zea Island anymore. As she gathered her belongings and tucked them into her satchel, she turned back to the elvor. "What about the island defenses?"

"What?"

"The island defenses. The magical barrier around the island." The last time the island had been under attack, a magical bubble had kept them from being harmed. Now that she was more awake, she wondered why that same barrier hadn't saved the fey from petrification.

"I wonder," Corran answered cryptically. "The barrier is still in place, that much is certain. However, there are some things that the barrier cannot protect against."

"What kinds of things?"

"Natural things."

"What does that mean?"

"It means that we have been under the assumption that it was a spell or similar method that has been turning people to stone. If the barrier did nothing to prevent it from occurring here, that can only mean that it was a natural ability rather than a casting that caused the petrification."

"Natural ability? You mean, like a basilisk?" She had recently seen a movie that featured such a creature. Although she hadn't considered the possibility of basilisks being real, it made sense. Even if they had been locked away just as the minotaurs had been, it was entirely possible that they had been released as well. She really needed to stop assuming that all of the mythical creatures known to the world were nothing more than legend. She knew firsthand how wrong that assumption could be.

"Could be a basilisk," Corran agreed. "I had understood them to be extinct but it is possible that one or more could have survived."

"But that doesn't quite make sense either. These attacks have been happening out in the human world too. Wouldn't people notice if a big lizard was chasing after them?"

"Big lizard?" The elvor turned a raised eyebrow in her direction. "Whatever makes you think that a basilisk is a big lizard?"

"I..." she stammered. "I think I saw it in a movie. So it's not a big lizard, then. What does it look like?"

"Basilisks are snakes," he explained. "Similar to the cuélebre you brought to us recently, without the wings and not quite as large. But they do have a crest atop their heads which appears to be similar to a crown."

"A big snake. That could totally move through the human world without being seen."

"Plus, you're forgetting something, like you always do." A tiny form, unnoticed as it crept through the trees while they spoke, dropped onto her shoulder, causing Morgan to shriek in surprise. "Basilisks are fey, just like Corran and I are. Don'cha remember what I taught you about fey glamour?"

"You're right, I'd forgotten. Fey can only be seen by humans when they want to be seen. So even if the basilisk had been a giant lizard instead of just a snake, the humans still wouldn't have noticed it there unless it wanted to be seen."

"Exactly. Now can we get going already? This place is starting to give me the creeps."

As much as Morgan wanted to stay put and help her friends, she knew that there was nothing on the island that would put things back to right. Until she, or someone else, found something that would turn the statues of her friends back to the people she loved, there was nothing for her to do there.

"There is a further reason why I am sending

you back to your world," Corran explained. "There has been some trouble with Liore and she needs to be distanced from the humans for a period."

Morgan was surprised that Liore was having trouble. Of all the things in her life, the last thing she thought she would need to be worried about was the shapeshifting elvor. "What happened?"

"I have not yet gathered all of the details. But it appears that her ordeal involves an altercation with other humans."

"Altercation?"

"That means she got in a fight," Tilson supplied. "A couple of the other girls in your class were picking on her. They didn't realize that Liore's pretty tough and can more than take care of herself."

Morgan could hardly imagine the elvor getting into a fight. She had always seemed so mild-mannered. "How did that happen?"

"I am certain she will be able to supply the details once you arrive," Corran stopped Tilson before he could answer. "For now, I believe your ride, as you call it, is here."

The gryphon-shaped shadow flickered across the ground as Askel circled high overhead, just at the very beginning of his descent. Morgan let out a sigh of relief that she hadn't even been aware that she'd been holding. "You're okay," she smiled at her friend as soon as he was on the ground and trotting toward them. "I was worried something had happened to you too."

"Worry not," he assured her, ducking his head so that she could run her hands across the feathers on his neck. "I am fine. I am relieved to see that you are well also."

"Yeah." Morgan took one last glance at the silent fey statues in the clearing. "I just wish they were okay, too."

"I have faith that you will come up with the means by which to restore them," he assured her as they took to the air. "You have not yet let us down."

"I know. But this seems like a much harder problem to solve."

"That's why it's your problem," Tilson yawned. "You're smart so you'll think of a good solution in no time."

Morgan blinked down at the haltija in surprise. "Was that a compliment?"

"What?" he shot upwards, almost standing in his indignation. His tail twitched back and forth and even the buffeting wind couldn't explain the twitching of his whiskers. "I would never."

"But you did," she grinned at him. "You said I was smart."

He continued to huff and puff, proclaiming that he would never have complimented her, the entire flight to Morgan's house. Askel even got a good chuckle out of the dispute but refrained from joining in.

"When will you come back?" As Morgan helped the still-protesting haltija from Askel's back, she had to ask the question that had been on her mind the entire flight. "How long am I supposed to just stay here?"

"I do not know. Hopefully I will return before too much time has passed." Her mouth twisted to the side, clearly demonstrating that she had much less faith in his assertion than he seemed to have, a motion that drew a chuckle from the gryphon. "You know. Liore isn't the only reason you were sent home."

"What do you mean?"

"Corran is worried for you. When he called for me, I had never heard him in such a state."

She had to admit that Corran's response to the devastation on Zea Island had been remarkable. Despite his normal calm and somewhat cold demeanor, he had seemed genuinely concerned for the first time since Morgan had met him. Perhaps there was more to him than she had initially believed. Additionally, she had been wearing her amulet the whole time he had been there and it hadn't made the slightest indication that he was being anything less than honest with what he had said.

Everything that had made sense in her world only days previously no longer made any sense at all. And now everyone was waiting on her to figure out a way to put everything back to the way it was supposed to be.

She just hoped she was up to the task.

~ 12 ~

HUMAN PROBLEMS

"It's that little twit, Brittany," Liore explained as she cleaned up the mess in Morgan's room in preparation to leave. "I put some notes on what's going on in the journal, but the short explanation is that she's just plain being a jerk and the next time she gets in my face, I'm gonna knock the pretty right out of her."

"What does that mean?"

"She's some sort of model on social media, so she thinks that all of the people she has following her on there give her some sort of power over everyone out here... or something like that."

"Seriously?"

Liore nodded. "It's really dumb but it doesn't seem to matter how much I ignore her, she just keeps coming after me."

"What is she so upset about?"

"She just plain doesn't like me," the elvor explained. "Well, us, I suppose. She doesn't like us. It started with Nathan but I don't really think he's the whole problem here."

Morgan wasn't entirely surprised that Brittany and her friends had continued to be a problem for Liore but she had hoped that her friend would have decreased some of the tension in her absence. From the sound of things, however, it seemed as though the opposite had happened. "I thought you said you could handle that."

Liore sighed in equal parts frustration and resignation. "I thought I could," she admitted. "But apparently, I was wrong. Those girls are just plain stubborn."

"Okay, so what exactly happened? Did something lead up to the fight you guys got into?"

"I really don't know. I mean, sure, they'd been obnoxious for a while but then they just started going really overboard. They started following me back to your house from school. That was fine, we both know I can just disappear whenever I want. But then they started following me from class to class, taking stuff out of my backpack and putting... other things... in."

"Other things? Like what kind of things?"

"Like an open can of soda, which got everywhere. That one made one heck of a mess, took forever to clean up. Then there was the dead mouse. That was fun, let me tell you. I guess they thought I'd have a problem with it, and they really didn't like it when I put it right back in their stuff. But I think the creepiest thing they shoved in there was a rock that looked like someone tried to carve it."

"Why was the rock creepy?"

Rather than answering, Liore picked up a small box that had been sitting on Morgan's desk. When she handed it over, Morgan looked inside, curious. Instead of just a randomly-shaped stone with chipping marks in it, the rock that had Liore so up in arms was far more sinister.

It was about four inches tall, not very big as

far as rocks go, but this one was definitely special. It hadn't just been carved by some random amateur, either. It was clearly a representation of Morgan herself. "What do you think this was about?"

The elvor shrugged. "Beats me. At first, I thought it might have something to do with the petrification attacks you've been investigating, like they knew about them somehow. But I don't see how that could be possible, as none of the other humans seem to have the slightest clue what's going on."

Morgan pondered her words as she turned the figurine over in her hands. "This seems a little too familiar," she said finally, "and a lot too much to just be a coincidence." She looked back up to meet her friend's eyes. "Remember the last figurine you gave me?"

"Yeah, the one Leander made. But this is totally different."

"Oh, I know. This one's rock, that was wood. This one's me, that one was Avekaine. But there are definite similarities here that I can't just ignore." She tucked the figure back into its box and set it down on the desk once more. "When you get back to the island, let Corran know about this too, would you?"

"Sure. Anything else you want me to pass along?"

"Just be careful. The island isn't safe, so make sure you watch your back, okay?"

"You know it. But I don't think that these girls are nearly as dangerous as whatever is causing these attacks, so you be sure to watch your own back too, got it?"

As her friend disappeared into the shadows cast by the wooded area behind her house, Morgan settled onto her bed to think. The similarities between the stone in the box and the carved wooden figure that she had returned to Leander were strong but not strong enough to override the possibility of coincidence. It was definitely suspicious and probably meant something more than what had already been read into it, she just couldn't think of what it meant right then.

The rock was still on her mind as she made her way to class the next morning. Just as Liore had warned her, Brittany and her friends followed her from the street into the school, jeering at her and trying to get close enough to cause problems. Having grown adept over the last few months at staying more than an arm's reach away from danger, Morgan just sidestepped the girls' attempts and settled into her seat.

Her mind was still too full of thoughts about the fey to pay much attention in class. She pulled out a piece of paper and sketched absently on it as she thought, watching as the form of Arien took shape. Even though she had seen him with her own eyes, she still could hardly believe that the apotharni had been turned to stone. Drawing had always soothed her in the past, so she hoped it would serve the same purpose now.

While she drew, she kept an eye on Nathan from the corner of her eye. It had been some time since she had seen him, and she wasn't sure how she was supposed to react now that she was back. Would he notice that it was her instead of Liore? Had he even noticed that she wasn't herself while she was away? Since he was fey himself, surely he would recognize a fey when it stood in front of him, wouldn't he?

The flying wad of paper that splatted against

the side of her face took her by surprise. She reached up to wipe away the wet mass, looking around the room suspiciously as she did so. She didn't have to look far to know who the culprits were, as Brittany and her friends were giggling and whispering among themselves, looking pointedly in her direction the whole time.

If they thought they would get a reaction out of her by their display, they were sure to be disappointed. Given some of the messy situations she had recently found herself in, a solitary spitwad was nowhere near enough of a threat. Of course, that didn't mean that she was above a little bit of revenge of her own. As the instructor continued to explain the lesson and draw on the whiteboard, she kept the girls in her peripheral vision, not wanting to be caught by surprise again, and turned her mind to payback. She knew it was petty and that she was just using the obnoxious girls as a target for all of the frustration she had been feeling lately but on the other hand, she didn't care. If they didn't want a fight, they probably shouldn't have picked one with her. Or Liore, for that matter.

She still hadn't come up with a good plan of retaliation that didn't seem overboard by the time class let out for lunch. Nathan, his trademark shy smile directed squarely at her, made a beeline for Morgan as soon as they were free. "You have finally returned," he said. "I had begun to wonder how long you would be gone."

She smiled at him in return, partly just because she was genuinely happy to see him but even more because he had noticed her absence. Of course he had known, she reminded herself. He's the Mirror Man, after all. He'd probably been watching over her the whole time she was gone.

"How go things with the fey?"

Her smile faltered at his question. "Not good," she admitted. "We still haven't found what's been causing the petrification, so we don't have any way to stop it." She explained how Zea Island had been attacked as well, causing her early return to the human world.

"What have you uncovered so far? Anything I may be of assistance with?"

"I'm not really sure. We discovered that at least one minotaur has gotten free, so that led to a whole discussion with Arien about the First Council. I assume you know who they are?"

"I do indeed. And I am very sorry to hear of what happened to your friends on the island."

"You know about that?" She looked up at him in surprise. "If you know what did it, tell me!"

He shook his head. "I overheard you telling Liore about it upon your return. Unfortunately, the culprit is as much a mystery to me as it is to you."

Disappointed, she turned back to her lunch. "As far as I can tell, fey who want to keep their world completely separate from that of the humans could pose a pretty big problem, particularly if they were letting all of their nasties out to wreak havoc out here. I know that there are still some fey out there who don't like humans, like Volcan, the minotaur, pretty much all the centaurs, and even some that I've worked directly with, like that dryad Meliai I met a few months ago."

"What about the man calling himself Meister Bas-Grann? I had overheard that he may be connected to all of this as well."

"I don't know," she shrugged. "I'm really

starting to wonder whether Bas-Grann is related to that group at all. I haven't seen anything that connects him to these attacks, but they kinda feel like they're his style."

"All right. So what else do you have?"

"Well, Corran and I talked about the possibility of a basilisk causing the petrification. I hadn't realized those were real things until just a few days ago." She twisted her mouth to the side. "I guess I should have known better."

"But you do not seem convinced of that."

"No," she shook her head. "Not completely. I mean, it's the best guess I've got right now, but it just... it doesn't feel right."

"Why not?"

"I understand that a snake can creep through human areas without being spotted, we already know about tons of snakes that do that all the time. But how can a basilisk get to all of the places where these attacks happened? Plus, Corran said that they were extinct. That would have to mean that not only is he wrong about that but there's more than one basilisk out there attacking people. Either that, or that there's something else behind all this."

"I see." He blinked his crystal-blue eyes at her. "That is a definite possibility. Basilisks are still much more numerous than most people realize. Despite what you have heard, they are not extinct. And while I agree with your statement that snakes can hide anywhere, they have the added advantage of using fey glamour."

"So you think it might be a basilisk, or more than one basilisk, after all?" Somewhat deflated, she set down her lunch. "It just..." she searched for the right words. "It just doesn't feel quite right, I guess. There's something I'm still missing; I just don't know what it is yet."

"Okay," he agreed. "Are there any more pieces of the puzzle that you hadn't considered yet?"

"I don't know." She thought for a long moment. "There is one other thing, but I'm not really sure what to make of it yet."

"What is that?"

"I think someone in the Zea Island council is a traitor. At least, it really seems that way."

Nathan's eyes widened at her statement. "Who do you suspect of this? Or is it a general feeling?"

"I hate to say it," she turned her eyes down as she spoke, "but I think it might be Corran. He's always so closed-off, it's really hard to tell what he's thinking. Plus he's pretty much the only one who didn't get turned to stone." She looked back up to meet his gaze. "If you knew an attack was coming, you'd get out of range, right?"

He pursed his lips and thought quietly about her question. "Is that the only reason you suspect him? If so, one could make the same assertion about you." Before she could protest, he raised a hand. "I am not saying it is you, of course, only that the argument could be made."

She had to admit that he was right. If not being petrified was cause for suspicion, she would be under suspicion as well. "I have other reasons," she explained quietly, "but I'm not sure I'm ready to explain any of them yet."

"I see." Finished with his own meal, he stood to leave, extending a hand to her to help her to her feet. "When you are ready, I am willing to listen. I'll not pressure you before then."

The rest of the day was normal, with teachers handing out instruction on topics with which

Morgan was unfamiliar. She really needed to figure out how to stay a bit more on top of what was being taught in class, she realized. At least there wasn't a test coming up for her to fail on.

The walk home from school was lonely. While out working with the fey, she normally had Tilson and often Askel as well. While living as a normal human, she had gotten used to having Nathan around but he had been called from class before school let out and wasn't able to walk her home. The loneliness she felt as she walked was far preferrable to the alternative, she realized, as a trio of unwelcome companions joined her.

"You need to stay out of our way," Brittany announced as she stepped up next to Morgan. "Otherwise you'll end up getting hurt pretty soon."

"I have no clue what you're talking about," Morgan answered in a bored voice. She wasn't interested in giving either her or her friends the satisfaction of knowing how annoyed they made her.

"She's talking about Nathan," Crystal, one of Brittany's cronies, explained. "You should know he's too good for you, so why don't you just leave him alone so that he can be with someone better?"

"Why don't you go find someone on your own instead of harassing me about my friends?" The irritation Morgan felt was finally beginning to show in her voice. She already knew that Brittany was interested in Nathan and although there wasn't anything beyond friendship currently between Nathan and Morgan, she wasn't about to let the other girl have him. "He's the one who can find someone better than you. In fact, I'd say the same thing about pretty much anyone who catches any of your eyes." She included all three girls in her insult, looking from Brittany on one side to Crystal and Jessica on the other.

"Just you wait," Jessica promised, "once everything we've been working on comes to pass, you'll be begging for us to let you say you knew us."

"Everything you're working on?" Morgan asked doubtfully. "And what would that be?"

"Brittany is already famous," Crystal explained, "but she's about to be a lot more famous here pretty soon. And I'm going to be a movie star too, just you watch."

Brittany nodded. "And Jessica is going to be a famous musician, too. And you'll just be stuck on the sidelines, paying for tickets to come see any of us." She smirked and added, "All we have to do is get you out of our way."

All three of the girls tittered in amusement but Morgan didn't get the joke. "I don't understand," she said finally. "What makes you think anyone'd pay to see any of you? Seems more like they'd pay you to stay away." She looked from one girl to the next. "I mean, I'd pay you to stay away. How much?"

"Why you little..." Jessica screeched in rage, but Crystal caught her before she reached Morgan.

"Don't let her get to you," Crystal said to her friend. "Pretty soon, she's going to be nobody at all."

"Less than nobody," Brittany agreed.

"She's going to be so completely out of the picture that nobody will even remember she was ever here. Like she's nothing more than one of these little statues everywhere." The trio fell back, giggling at their own private joke, while Morgan continued to walk down the street toward her house.

"What was that all about?" Morgan fumed once she was securely inside her own bedroom. "I get it. You want Nathan. But seriously? Movie star? Musician?" She dropped her backpack next to her desk. While she had homework that needed to be done, there were other studies that were higher priority, at least in her mind. "What makes any of them think they'll get famous?" She dug through her closet and pulled out her spellbook. "Especially with attitudes like those."

Suddenly, one of the comments the vile girls had made sank into her brain. "Like one of the statues?" She shot to her feet, book in hand but forgotten for the moment. "Did they really say that?" Liore's comment that the girls seemed to know more than the rest of the human population rose in her mind and her eyes slid over to land on the box that loomed on her desk, the box containing the small carved rock figurine. Their comment had been just vague enough to be coincidental, but she didn't believe it. There were simply too many things for it to have been made purely by chance.

"It's not even about Nathan," she recognized finally. "They've got to be involved in the petrification somehow." The only thing that made sense, even though she didn't quite understand how it could be true, was that Brittany and her friends were somehow involved with Bas-Grann.

"I mean, he was a human, after all, so he probably understands humans pretty well. And if he can offer them power, they'd be likely to accept it. It's like they made a deal with the devil." A deal, one that could make all their wishes come true, would explain their certainty that they would all become famous. It was probably a good thing that Liore had been sent home. If the girls were to uncover the truth about her shapeshifting abilities, as unlikely as such a discovery would be, that could cause real trouble for Morgan. "So what do I do about them?"

Still grumbling to herself, she settled down to research her magic. She was trying to develop the habit of studying her magic after school every day, just as she had been while

Arien had been teaching her. Today, however, she was too annoyed at the trio to pay much attention. The sigils just swirled meaninglessly across the page.

"I have some news for you." Nathan's arrival startled her enough to make her jump from her bed. Her spellbook fell to the floor and she hurriedly picked it up.

She wasn't sure if it would hurt any of the magic if the book got damaged but she decided it was better to be safe than sorry. "What kind of news?"

"About the centaurs," he explained as he helped her pick up the assortment of papers that had scattered along with the book. "It would appear that you riled them a bit more than anticipated."

Morgan remembered the centaurs a little too well. She stole the amulet that they used to determine their clan leader, not because she had wanted the amulet or to take leadership for herself but because the amulet was actually a part of the Cup of Jamshid, a magical item that she had borrowed the first time meeting the Mirror Man. The Cup, she remembered, that Corran had wanted her to hand over to him so that he could return it to Fantas. Normally she would have taken the elvor up on his offer, as she had every other time she had "borrowed" an item from someone that required returning, but that had been the same time she had discovered he was lying to her about returning items to their proper owners.

"What's up with the centaurs?" she asked as she settled her notes onto her desk.

"They are angry with you," he explained. "Angry enough to have joined forces with the one called Meister."

"Seriously?" She looked up at him, horrified at his news. Although the possibility of the fey working with Ameil Bas-Grann had occurred to her, she had mostly dismissed the idea. Now, it would appear she had been wrong. Totally wrong. Her stomach sank into her feet as she considered what this would mean, not just for her but also for the rest of the fey.

Nathan nodded slowly. "My news grows worse, I am afraid. The leader of the centaurs has vowed revenge upon you personally for the theft of his amulet. Once that was taken, he was forced to fight anew to retain his standing among the tribe, a fight he seems unwilling to forgive."

Morgan nodded slowly. "I should have known he'd still be miffed about that." If she was in his position, she'd probably be pretty angry too. If he was this angry with her, at the very least, perhaps he wouldn't take his wrath out on the rest of her friends. Not that she had many of them left for him to target. "How bad is it?"

"I do not currently know the extent of his wrath, but many centaurs passed into the ether in the combat for dominance." Clouds covered his eyes at the words, shifting Morgan's focus.

"How many?" her voice was much softer this time.

"Too many," he answered. "Though I am saddened by the loss of more fey, I am hopeful that the diminished quantity of centaurs will mean that you will remain safe for a period longer."

"Me too," she agreed. The last thing she needed right then was angry centaurs bent on vengeance for the theft. She already had enough problems to deal with.

LOTHAR

The next afternoon, Morgan received another surprise visitor. This one didn't arrive through the front door, as Nathan had, but instead arrived at her bedroom window, hovering in the air just outside. Morgan smiled as she recognized the friendly face of Leander.

"Leander! It's great to see you, how have you been?"

Years previously, Leander had been a chosen, just as Morgan currently was. He worked with the same fey on the same council as Morgan, so the pair had quite a lot in common. The biggest difference, besides just the few years in age, was that Leander had been removed as a chosen when he fell in love with an elvor maiden.

Avekaine, the elvor maiden, had refused her betrothal to an elvor man due to her feelings for Leander. When they discovered it was a human rather than an elvor for whom she had such feelings, her family, Corran included, forced her to return home, leaving Leander behind. Leander was returned to the world of the humans as a result, all memories of his time with the fey erased. His memories didn't return until he heard the wailing of Avekaine's spirit, trapped at the place where she died.

Leander's history with the fey had caused some initial confusion and conflict between the two humans, a conflict that Morgan had dropped when she discovered Leander hadn't been a threat to them after all. His only goal had been putting Avekaine's spirit to rest. That didn't mean that all of his animosity toward the fey had disappeared but he had rebuilt his friendship with most of them. With the exception of Corran, who was Avekaine's cousin and who had caused Leander's removal, all of the fey accepted Leander as a presence within their world.

"Not good," he explained as he climbed in through her window. "I didn't know who else to turn to. I tried to go to Zea Island, but they've all been..." his voice faltered and he raised a hand to cover his mouth, as though to refuse what he was trying to say.

"I know." Morgan helped him inside and settled him onto the chair in front of her desk. "I was there when it happened."

"So you know what did that?"

She shook her head. "I've been trying to understand it myself." His agitation had to be more than just from what had happened on the island, so she took a step back and looked at him critically. "Did something happen with the druids?" Leander had been studying with a pair of druids in order to become one himself, so he hadn't been around to visit for quite some time. In fact, the only time Leander had even come up in conversation was when Liore had mentioned she was heading out to meet him while Morgan stayed at home to study her magic.

"No," he shook his head. "They're not. I need to reach Stormshock right away."

Morgan blinked at him in surprise. "You don't know how to contact him?"

"No. I was hoping you would. That's why I'm here."

Morgan's brows creased as she considered the situation. "I don't have any way to contact him either," she explained finally. "But if there's anything I can do to help, I'm more than willing to try."

"That would be great," he sighed in relief. "Hopefully you can make some sense out of all this."

Morgan looked out the window, concerned. "I don't know how to get there, though. I always ride with Askel, or sometimes Vouivre, but I can't call on either of them right now. How am I supposed to get out to the Biscayan territories?"

"You know me," he smiled sadly as he pulled a necklace out of his pocket and offered it to her. "Always here to help." The necklace was identical to the one he currently wore, which had allowed him to hover outside her window, even on the second story. "I actually made this for you a while ago so you could travel when you needed to instead of relying on everyone else all the time. Thought it might come in handy."

Morgan had borrowed his necklace in the past, so she knew how to use it. After grabbing her own supplies, she slipped the chain over her head, tucking it next to her own amulet and followed him out into the sky.

"So what am I getting into?" she asked as they flew. "You haven't even told me what's going on yet."

"I haven't?" Surprise crossed his face. "Sorry, I guess my brain's still a bit messy right now. Given what I saw at the island, I can only assume you know about the petrification attacks, correct?" When she nodded, he continued. "They've been happening out where I was, too. Tellius and Lothar were looking into them as well; it seems like everyone's been searching for answers here."

"I hadn't heard that they were happening everywhere," Morgan answered, "but it makes a lot of sense that other people would be looking for answers too."

"Tellius and Lothar thought the stone attacks looked a lot like those done by a woman named Eurale a long time ago." As though sensing her objection, he raised a hand. "I know, she'd be long since dead by now. So they don't think it was actually her out there doing this but they do think it was someone like her, someone who learned her tricks somewhere."

"We were thinking along the lines of a basilisk," Morgan offered. "I've never even heard of this Eurale person before."

"I believe it," he chuckled. "In fact, I hadn't heard about her either until the guys started telling me all this stuff about her. But I'd bet you've heard of her sister."

"Sister?"

"Yep. In fact, there were three of them. One of them is by far the most famous, though. Her name was Medusa."

Morgan's jaw fell at the news and she almost fell from the sky in surprise. "Medusa? You mean from the Greek legend, Medusa? Turns people into stone by looking at them Medusa?"

He nodded. "Same one. Apparently her ability to petrify people was some sort of a curse, so the guys were thinking that someone else out there may have ended up with the same thing. They just haven't figured out how."

"But..." she faltered. Her brain was still trying to make sense of the whole situation. "That was hundreds of years ago. She's just a legend..." she stopped as she recognized how ridiculous she sounded. How long was she going to keep protesting that things couldn't po9ssibly be real because she had believed them to just be a myth? "So how are we supposed to find this person, if they really are out there?"

"I'm not sure," Leander answered, "but that's not the problem I was looking for help with. That was just what caused the problem I got stuck on."

"You're not making sense again."

"I know," he chuckled. "But bear with me, I'm almost there." He took a deep breath, one that appeared to be much more difficult than it should have been. Morgan wondered whether whatever had happened had hurt him in some

way. Before she could ask, however, he continued his explanation.

"Tellius found an item, one that was designed to protect him against petrification spells, which he figured would work against this type of thing. Whether it's a spell or an ability, it all has the same effect, so if he's protected against the effect, he's protected against the cause. With me so far?"

"Yeah."

"He took this item, I don't actually know what it was, and headed out to stop the attacks. Apparently he figured out where they were coming from and decided to confront the problem at the source. When he didn't come back, Lothar and I went out to look for him. Lothar had a tracking spell on Tellius so that he'd know where he was."

"Good idea."

"Well, yes and no. We found him, at least for the most part. By the time we got there, whatever he had been after was long gone but he was still there." He swallowed deeply before adding, "unless we find out a way to fix all this, he's going to be there for a long time."

Morgan blinked as dawning grew. "He got turned to stone." It wasn't a question, as she could see the answer clearly written across her friend's face. "So is that where we're headed?"

Leander shook his head. "Lothar brought him back to the grove, so we're headed there. He'd hoped that someone found a way to reverse the effects already but now I have to tell him that we don't have a cure yet."

Morgan felt for both his situation and Lothar's. She would love to have been able to say she had a solution to their problem, to her own problems too, but she just hadn't managed to come up with any answers yet. They flew in silence for the rest of the journey, only talking when it was necessary.

While they traveled, she reflected back on some of the strange turns and twists her friendship with Leander had taken. She was only just learning how to be a chosen, having been brought to the world of the fey fairly recently when she had met him. He, in turn, was still regaining the memories of his own time among the fey, memories that had been taken at Corran's orders when Leander was removed as chosen. The first handful of encounters between the current and previous chosen were hostile, with him trying to achieve his own goals, goals which had initially seemed counter to Morgan's own goals. Eventually they had come to a mutual understanding and then developed a friendship, one that had served both of them well on multiple occasions. Whenever one of them was in need, the other was sure to come running to the rescue.

They came in for a landing in the small grove of trees, the same grove that Morgan had once sheltered within to get away from a storm. That had been when she had first met the druids who lived there, the same druids who had given her the cloak that had saved her life, as well as the staff and amulet she carried with her everywhere. Much as she wanted to go directly to Lothar, the motionless form of Tellius drew her closer.

She had grown since she had last seen the friendly druid, she discovered. The expression on his face was nothing that she had ever seen on him before, a mixture of fear and anger. His left arm was outstretched, as though willing the attack to not strike him. Tears welled up in her eyes as she looked up into his face, knowing that he didn't even realize she was there. It was the same feeling she had felt when looking upon what remained of Arien.

"I don't have anything to fix him," she said quietly to Lothar. "And I have no idea what caused this."

Lothar raised both hands and began gesturing. He couldn't speak, which she had learned the first time they met, but he could hear everything. While Morgan had learned a few gestures of his language, there was no way for her to follow what he was saying at that moment.

"He knows you don't have the answers," Leander translated. "He's just glad to see that you're still alive and well." He continued to explain that Lothar was mad at himself for not being there when Tellius needed him and not having anything more to offer as a result.

She wiped the tears from her cheeks and looked around, spotting for the first time the pair of foals on the edge of the clearing. Unlike regular horses, these had tiny wings growing out of their shoulders. "Is that a pegasus?"

Leander nodded and smiled, gesturing clearly for her to follow him closer. "We've been working with a group of pegasi lately," Leander explained. "These were born just a week ago so they can't fly yet. That's why they're still here."

"They're beautiful," Morgan breathed as she ran a hand over their soft fur. "And so tiny!"

"Not for much longer," Leander chuckled. "Horses tend to grow pretty fast and pegasus foals grow even faster. These will be full-sized in about a month or so."

"Why are they here?" She looked up at the men. "I mean, if they were just born a few days ago, shouldn't they be with their mother?"

Lothar nodded. "Their mother was killed by some sort of hunter. They have been entrusted to us for their safekeeping until they are old enough to travel." He looked from the foals to the sky as a shadow crossed the ground. "Speaking of which, here comes their father now."

A massive black winged stallion gracefully landed, folded his wings against his sides, and trotted over to nuzzle the foals.

"We should leave them," Leander suggested. "They are still in mourning as well."

Morgan was absolutely appalled, not just at what had become of her friend but at what had happened to the pegasus mare as well. Her amulet let her understand what the stallion was saying to his children, words to the effect that he would seek out whoever had done this to their mother and exact his own revenge for all of them. She could understand the sentiment.

"I will do everything I can," she looked from Leander to Tellius to the small group of pegasi, "to find out who is responsible for this. Not just to find them, but to put a stop to all of this. No matter what it costs."

~ 14 ~

HIGH COUNCIL

While Morgan was still getting settled into the grove with Lothar and Leander, a small group of peri came to see her. They were agitated, unusually so, even for peri. Initially, Morgan assumed that their concern was about Tellius, or perhaps about the pegasi, but she quickly discovered that neither of those was the cause.

"It's the Mirror Man," one of them explained as she hovered in front of Morgan's face.

"Yes, the Mirror Man," another echoed.

"Yes, I know he's been missing for a while now." That news had spread long ago, so she didn't see why the peri were still so concerned over his absence.

"No, that's not what we meant," the first one said.

"Well, not exactly," the second one added.

"He's missing, yes, but he's missing twice." Both peri nodded at the words, as though that statement should somehow make sense.

"What do you mean, missing twice?"

"Well, he was missing," the first peri said.

"But then he went missing from where he was missing to."

"Missing from where he was missing to? How does that work?" A sinking feeling began to spread through Morgan's stomach at their words. She had a bad feeling about all this.

"He went missing into the human world."

"He wanted to hide among the humans."

"Because he looks like a human."

"He's not just an Ancient, he's a human too."

"Okay, so what about it?" She wasn't sure how the peri had discovered where Nathan was hiding but if any of the fey were to uncover his location, it would have been the peri.

"He's missing from the human world too."

"The Meister found him. His people took him away."

"They attacked him just a few hours ago. We only just heard the news."

"Nobody knows where they've taken him to."

Morgan sat back, stunned. She had agreed with Nathan that the human world would be the safest place for him to hide out, but now it appeared that they had both been wrong. She wondered if somehow the attack on Tellius had been intentional to draw her away from him so that he could be taken. If that was the case, not only had their tactic worked beautifully, it had cost her one of her friends in the process. That idea gnawed at her, festering in her stomach and adding more fuel to the fires of anger that continued to grow.

Even worse, as she considered how many had already been attacked, she wondered whether she would be able to save any of her friends at all. Almost everyone around her had been turned to stone and the ones that remained were still under threat. The only reason she wasn't already howling in frustration was due to the presence of Leander and Lothar, who she was positive didn't need any more stress at that moment. They were two of the last people she still had, at least those who were still alive and able to walk around on their own.

"I need to go back home," she finally explained to Leander when the peri were done chattering. "I need to figure out what happened to the Mirror Man."

Both of the druids looked at her, matching expressions of shock on their faces. "You know who the Mirror Man is?"

She nodded. "Yeah. He and I got to be friends a while ago, so I've been keeping an eye on him while he was in the human world."

Leander appeared mortified at the news. "If I'd known you were guarding an Ancient, I wouldn't have brought you all the way here."

"It's not your fault," she waved his concern away. "He's capable enough, at least I think he is. Plus, he's an Ancient. Just because nobody knows where he is, that doesn't automatically mean he's been taken." At least, she hoped that was the case. It felt like false optimism but it was all she had at that moment.

"I'll go with you," he said after a brief

conversation with Lothar. "Lothar says he has things under control here but now he's more worried about the Mirror Man."

"Okay," she agreed. "Let's go."

The flight from her house to the druids' grove had taken a very long time, given how worried Morgan had been about what they would find there. The flight back to her house, on the other hand, made their previous journey seem instantaneous. Her imagination ran wild with thoughts of what could have happened to Nathan, of finding his statue upon their return. Part of her didn't want to go, knowing how upset she would be to see that, but the bigger part of her knew she had no choice. She needed to go. She needed to see, to confirm with her own eyes what had befallen her friend.

As though sensing there was more to her reaction than just that of a chosen safekeeping an Ancient, Leander kept an eye on her throughout the flight but made no effort at conversation. More than once, it appeared as though he wanted to ask questions but never quite brought himself to do so.

The first place they went was to Morgan's

house, a familiar location for both of them to start. Rather than coming in for a landing, however, she headed toward a small house a few blocks away, where Nathan had been living while in the human world. They didn't have to worry about parents or other humans seeing them, stopping them to question what they were up to, as Nathan lived alone without adult guidance, just as he had done in the world of the fey.

She came in for a hard landing on Nathan's front porch, almost crashing into his front door in the process. More experienced in using the flying necklace and less agitated by what may be waiting for them, Leander stepped gracefully out of the air next to her. Undeterred by her own lack of flying expertise, Morgan first tried the knob then, once determining it was locked, began to bang on the door, shouting Nathan's name.

"Want me to open it?" Leander suggested. "I have a spell for that."

Morgan scowled. Of course he had a spell for that. It seemed that he had a spell for everything she needed. If only she had a spell for that too. "Yeah, thanks."

"*Po'ort*," he said. With a soft click, the door unlatched and swung open.

Immediately, Morgan darted in through the opening, calling for Nathan again, hope of his response decreasing by the second. She checked in the living room, the kitchen, his bedroom, and even the bathroom before finally accepting that he simply wasn't home.

Even as she searched, she knew that she wouldn't find him. There was no reason for the peri to come tell her that he was missing from the human world if that hadn't been the case. She stopped in the middle of his living room and looked around, searching for any sign of him and where he could have gone.

Being in Nathan's home was just as disconcerting as it had been every other time she had been by to visit. Mirrors covered almost every inch of his walls and a handful of free-standing mirrors stood on the small table near the couch and on the long chest of drawers under the big window that faced his front yard. Unlike the mirrors he had used back in his keep, very few of the mirrors in his human home were covered by cloth. Given his nature, the mirrors were a necessary item. He used them to keep tabs on everything. None of them appeared to have been disturbed and there was no other evidence, at least none in plain view, of what had happened to him.

"What is all this?" Leander looked around in amazement. "It's like standing in the middle of a disco ball or something."

"Yeah," she agreed. "It was pretty uncomfortable at first, but you get used to it."

He stepped closer to one of the larger mirrors, examining his own reflection. "I guess it makes sense to have all of these, he is called the Mirror Man, after all." He turned to face Morgan again. "What's he like?"

She turned surprised eyes toward him. "You never met him?" When he only shook his head in response, she raised an eyebrow. Somehow it hadn't ever occurred to her that she had met someone Leander had not. She knew that he was familiar with the fey on Zea Island, and he had known Stormshock as well, but she had just assumed that he knew all of the fey she did. "I guess you wouldn't have," she finally admitted. "He said I was the first to come see him since he was really young."

Remembering her first encounter with the Mirror Man brought her back to the current situation with a sharp jolt. "You're right," she breathed. "He's the Mirror Man. If he's not a statue, that means he's out there somewhere."

"I think you lost me," Leander said. "What are you talking about?"

"The mirrors. He uses them to watch over everything."

"Well yeah, but what does that have to do with where he is now?"

"He doesn't just use them to watch," she explained. "He can use them to travel, too."

Leander's eyes widened at her words. "You mean he can walk through the mirror?"

"Exactly." She moved from mirror to mirror, wishing she knew how he activated them. As many times as she had seen him use the mirrors, she had never quite noticed how he got them to show what he wanted to see. Even the time she had used a mirror to go from his keep to Fantas's place, she hadn't understood how it worked. "I just need to figure out which one is the right one to use. I don't suppose you have a spell to activate one of these, do you?"

Leander shook his head, still obviously trying to wrap his mind around what she was saying. "So you think you can use one of these to contact him?"

"Maybe. If I can just figure out how to turn one on, it might show me where he is." She headed for a different mirror, continuing her search. "But the important thing is that he can go through at least one of them to get to safety. If he knew he was being targeted, that he had been found here, then chances are pretty good that he was able to use one of these to get out before he got grabbed."

She had nothing but faith to back up her ideas but the more she thought about it, the calmer she felt. Recognizing the subtle but unmistakable feeling of being watched, she whirled around, certain she would discover a pair of sapphire eyes observing her from one of the glass surfaces. To her dismay, the only thing revealed in the reflective surface was own disheveled appearance.

"There you are," a tiny voice called up from the floor. "I've been looking everywhere for you." Tilson climbed up her clothing to take his customary position on her shoulder.

"I was in the Biscayan Territories," she explained absently, still trying to figure out how to activate a mirror. "Tellius got attacked too."

"Tellius? The druid?"

"Yeah. Leander came and got me to take a look. Lothar's still with him, though."

"That's terrible news, just terrible," the haltija moaned. "But still, you gotta go. The council's looking for you."

Reluctant to give up the search but realizing that she wouldn't have been summoned if it wasn't for something important, she turned to Leander. "Can you stay here for a few?" she asked. "If he does come back, you can tell him what's going on."

Leander agreed so she and Tilson headed out. She would have much preferred to stay herself, to find Nathan and ensure he was okay, but that wasn't going to happen. When the council called, she had to go. There was no choice in the matter, no deliberation on her own preferences.

Besides, Tilson would get even more annoying than usual if she didn't get moving quickly. He was the most impatient fey she had ever met.

They walked back to her house where Askel waited for them. He, unlike Tilson, almost never showed signs of dissatisfaction at the amount of time between his arrival and Morgan's appearance. "Hey, Askel, how are you doing?" He had been a friend to everyone on Zea Island even longer than Morgan had, so he was sure to take the most recent attack personally. If anyone, she would have expected him to be the impatient one this time, not Tilson.

"I am pleased to see that you are still healthy," the gryphon explained as he lowered himself for her to climb onto his back. "And I still hold faith that this will all be resolved soon."

"Me too," she sighed as they took to the air, not sure she believed her own words. As they flew, she looked around. "Where are we going? Zea Island is the other way."

"We are not going there," he explained. "We are going to meet with the High Council."

Morgan was stunned. Sure, she had heard of the high council, the group of fey who watched over all of the other councils, such as the one on Zea Island. For a moment she wondered why they had summoned her but then she realized she already knew what this summons must be about. She was a chosen, tasked with watching over and helping the council and she had failed. While she had slept among them, her council had been turned to stone. Of course there would be fallout from that. She just hoped that when it was all over, she would still be a chosen and not be sent back home, her memories of them and her adventures erased as had been done with Leander. Even worse, of the three Ancients she had met, she had lost two and killed one. Her track record of safeguarding the fey was terrible. Lost in thought and certain of her fate, she barely paid any attention as they circled to land.

"Welcome," Stormshock's voice broke through her miserable spiral. "It is wonderful to see you again, although I believe we can all agree that these are not optimal circumstances."

She looked up in shock at the voice, wondering what she could possibly say to the massive emerald dragon in response to the questions he no doubt had. Only after a long breath did his words finally register.

"I'm not in trouble?" she asked as she slid from Askel's back to the stones on which he stood. The stones encircled a massive pool of water, inside which Stormshock lounged. Looking past the dragon, she spotted the familiar winding path that had once led to Zea Island.

"Of course not," he reassured her. "In fact, we are quite pleased that you have not fallen victim to these attacks as well."

When she had first become an emissary to the fey, Morgan had been intimidated by both the dragon's massive presence and his somewhat excitable nature. When he had been killed, she had been far more upset by the loss than by any of the other losses she and the rest of the fey had experienced at the time. The revelation that he was still alive continued to be a secret to most of the fey.

Looking around again, she realized that she, Askel, Tilson and Stormshock weren't the only ones in the grotto. The Irusan lounged on the opposite side of the pool, his massive size diminished in comparison to the massive dragon. Also in the water was a mermaid wearing a silvery helmet, a mermaid Morgan knew. "Nitsa?"

Nitsa, head of the underwater Ceara Temple, smiled at her in return. "It is good to see you once again, chosen."

Other fey that Morgan didn't know were there as well, but Morgan turned back to Stormshock. "What's going on? Why are we all here? Aren't you still hiding?"

"You knew?" Tilson finally spoke up, his voice carrying far more indignation than what his body should have been capable. "You knew he was still alive and you didn't tell me?"

"I wasn't allowed to," she explained. She could understand his response, she would probably have reacted the same way, had their positions been reversed.

"All will be explained shortly," Stormshock explained. "We are only waiting on one last arrival." Even as he spoke, Morgan spotted yet another familiar figure walking along the circular path, making his way to the grotto.

"My apologies for being late," Corran said calmly as he climbed the last few stones to join the group. "The entrance was more securely sealed than I had originally understood it to be." His eyes locked onto Stormshock as he crested the rocky mound and he almost lost his footing in surprise. Only Askel's quick reflexes as he reached out a stabilizing wing kept him from falling. "You are alive," Corran's voice was barely over a whisper. "We had believed you to be dead."

"As far as everyone outside this group knows, I am dead," Stormshock explained. "I had intended to keep it that way for a while longer yet to allow the passage of more time before my return but it appears that time is precisely the commodity in which we currently find ourselves in short supply. Thank you for joining us."

Corran settled into a seated position on the stones, looking back and forth between the no-longer-dead dragon and the unsurprised chosen. "Did you know?" he hissed at her.

Morgan simply nodded and shrugged her shoulder, not wanting to say anything that could anger the irate elvor any further than he already was. The normally cold and unperturbed elvor was practically bristling, something she hadn't ever considered seeing in him. That unsettled her much more than she expected. Was his response due to his failure to kill the dragon? She wondered. It seemed more as though there was relief mixed into his reaction, relief that wouldn't have been there had he been in any way responsible for the attacks.

"First of all, for those of you who have not already met her, may I introduce Morgan. She has been acting as chosen for the council of Zea Island, working closely with Corran for some time now."

The fey she knew nodded and smiled at her while those she didn't offered greetings and words of welcome. Even more taken aback than she had already been, Morgan wasn't sure how to respond.

"That is not why she is here today," the dragon continued. "Today, she is here as chosen. Not as the chosen of the Zea Island council, but as chosen of this council."

That announcement got a gasp of surprise from the crowd, the loudest of which came from Corran. "But that is..." he sputtered, "she is already a chosen. Nobody can be a chosen of more than one council, particularly a council such as this one!"

"We believe that Morgan is more than up to the task," Stormshock explained. "She has proven herself far worthier than any chosen we have had in a very long while."

"Would you have us find a different chosen, in that case? While you may believe her capable of being the chosen for two councils, I do not share your certainty. For one as inexperienced as her to be selected as the chosen for the High Council is unheard-of."

"You will not need to select a new chosen," the Irusan spoke up for the first time. "All will be explained in due time."

Recognizing that he had been overruled before he had even begun to object, Corran settled back down once more. The expression on his face, not to mention the narrowing of his eyes, told Morgan everything she needed to know about his thoughts on the matter.

~ 15 ~

ICE PRISON

Once all of the furor about Stormshock's return and Morgan's selection as chosen for the High Council, a decision Morgan herself wasn't altogether sure about, the discussion turned to other topics.

"As you all know by now, Corran has been speaker of the Zea Island council for some time," Stormshock spoke up. "Some have suggested that he should be promoted to a position within the High Council as a result of his actions within his own council. The last time we met, we voted on whether or not to admit him among our ranks. While that vote was not unanimous," he paused to look meaningfully around the group, his gaze lingering the longest on Corran himself, "the final decision was to approve his admission into the High Council."

This news surprised Morgan. Not so much that Corran had been considered as a member of the High Council, she had long suspected that was his goal, but that he had been voted in. Stormshock himself had told her that he believed not all members of the Zea Island council were trustworthy and she personally suspected the elvor of deception. After the attack that had turned almost the entire Zea Island council to stone, Corran had been one of the few who had survived the attack. It just seemed too suspicious for her to readily accept as mere coincidence. Perhaps she should have told Stormshock of her concerns after all.

"Today, he joins us as a full-fledged member of the High Council. Please join me in congratulating him."

She looked sidewards at Askel, trying to determine what the gryphon was thinking. As usual, the gryphon was impossible to read. After scrutinizing her friend's face, she turned her attention to Corran to see what he thought of this announcement. While she had fully expected him to appear pleased, which he did, she hadn't expected him to look so troubled. Why was he not more excited at the news that he had been accepted? Did her presence here really bother him so much that it undermined everything else?

"I believe the next thing we need to discuss," the Irusan pointed out, "is the missing Mirror Man." A murmur went through the group at that, most of whom seemed to agree that this topic warranted further conversation. "None have heard from him in months now and, while he has been known for his absence, this seems to be at odds with our current situation."

"He is not missing," Nitsa explained. "He has been hiding in the world of the Humans. Morgan has been in regular contact with him, helping to watch over him while he is there."

Attention returned to Morgan at that point, and she uncomfortably shuffled her feet. "Well yeah, he's been hiding out there. He moved just down the street from me. But he's not actually there anymore."

"What do you mean by this?" Corran demanded.

"He..." she searched for words again and finally shrugged. "He's not there anymore. I was actually at his house looking for him when Tilson came to let me know you guys wanted to meet with me."

"Do you have any ideas on where he may have gone?" Nitsa asked.

Morgan shook her head. "I know that he can travel through his mirrors, so I thought maybe he was able to escape when he found out someone discovered where he is. I just haven't been able to figure out where he went or how to contact him, wherever he is."

"He did not escape," Stormshock said. "He was taken by those working with Ameil Bas-Grann." He paused after that statement, correctly anticipating the outcry at his words.

"What do you mean he's been taken?"

"We must mount a rescue at once!"

"Where is he being held?"

"How was he taken from the human world? Did you not say he was to be safe there?"

"We do not know at this time how he was

taken, nor do we know where he is being held. We have confirmed that he is still alive, but that is all."

Morgan's heart sank at his words. Although the peri had told him Nathan was missing, that he had been taken, she had held onto the hope that he'd somehow managed to escape. The dragon's words dashed the last traces of hope she held to that end.

"We need to get him back," she said quietly. "We can't just let Ameil keep him like this."

"We are searching now for information on where he is being held and for a means of retrieving him." Stormshock directed the statement directly toward Morgan. "In the meantime, we have an assignment for you."

Morgan's brows furled. She wasn't interested in going out on assignment while Nathan was still missing but she had faith that Stormshock was doing all he could to find him. "What's the assignment?"

"You must go to Hoarfrost Castle."

A fresh uproar sounded from the gathered fey.

"You cannot send her there!"

"Are you joking? No humans are allowed at Hoarfrost Castle!"

"This is madness."

"You will be joined," Stormshock continued as though the protests had never been voiced, "by Tilson, as usual, and by Askel. Furthermore, Vouivre will join you."

This time, Corran joined the protests. "Vouivre is the most powerful fey I have left," he explained. "Should anything happen to him while he is on this assignment, Zea Island will be left completely defenseless!"

"I understand your concerns," the dragon turned his attention to the elvor, "but he is the best chance we have for Morgan to succeed. Without him, she is likely to fail. If she fails, we will all be left defenseless, not just Zea Island."

Corran's head snapped back at his words as though he had been physically attacked. "Who will guard Zea Island in his absence?"

"With the direct assault on your council, Zea Island has already fallen. We must now gather and redistribute our resources so that those of us who can still be saved are safeguarded to the best of our ability."

Silence fell across the grotto like a blanket of ice, sending a chill down Morgan's spine. Zea Island was lost? How could that possibly be? Was that what they had meant when they said they weren't worried about her answering to two councils? "What about the fey who were turned to stone?" she asked finally, her voice barely above a whisper.

"They have been transported for safekeeping," the Irusan explained. "Until we find a means by which to restore them, there is little else that we can do."

"We have sent word to Alberich," another of the gathered fey spoke up for the first time. "We had the idea that if anyone had the means to change stone to flesh, it would be the dvergar."

"And what came of that inquiry?"

The fey shook his head. "Nothing. We received a message that the dvergar could not help us and since they had withdrawn from the council, no further information would be shared. They respectfully request that we not contact them again."

Morgan remembered having heard the name earlier. Alberich was the king of the dvergar, the one who had called for a withdrawal from the council shortly after the petrification attacks had begun. She wasn't surprised that they didn't have a ready solution; had they known how to fix the problem, not only would that have been shared quite a while ago but the dvergar wouldn't have felt the need to retreat. Their request to be left completely alone, on the other hand, was a bit surprising.

"You swear to me," she looked each member of the High Council in the eye as she pushed herself to her feet and spoke loudly, "that you will look for the Mirror Man while I am gone, that you will do everything you can in order to release him. Swear this to me and I will go to this Hoarfrost Castle."

"Chosen or not, you don't get to make demands of this council," another of the gathered council members spoke up, but Nitsa interrupted him.

"Morgan has saved all of us more times than any other chosen before her. She stopped the attacks on the dragons when their ether had been trapped. She found a cure for the illness that threatened all of feykind. I have absolute faith that she will find a way to restore our petrified kin and save them as well. Her actions and her actions alone have led her to be selected as this council's chosen, so if anyone has a right to make such a demand upon us, it is her."

"We so swear." She smiled at Morgan as she did, and Morgan believed her.

"Well then," she turned to her friends, "we'd better get moving then."

Askel nodded his agreement and she climbed onto his back.

"Vouivre will catch up with you along the way," Stormshock said as the gryphon picked his way down the rocks. "Be careful, as we are all depending on you."

As they headed into the thin clouds overhead, Morgan was quiet, deep in thought. Despite the bravado she had shown to the council, she wasn't even close to being excited about this latest assignment. Hoarfrost Castle, whatever that was, sounded cold. She dug through her satchel to pull out a tiny ring studded with diamonds. Corran, by way of Tilson, had given it to her when she first became a chosen and it had already saved her life once. Now, she hoped it would do so again.

Assuming, of course, that Hoarfrost Castle was actually frozen. While most of the time, the fey called things by names that made sense, other times they were the complete opposite. If Hoarfrost Castle turned out to be in the middle of a desert or something similar to that, the ring would do little to help her.

"So why was everyone so afraid of this castle?" she asked. "Someone said that humans aren't allowed there. Why not?"

The gryphon let out a low whistle. "I am nervous for you to go there as well," he admitted. "It is a very dangerous place, designed to hold the most dangerous fey."

"What do you mean?"

Tilson, who had been oddly silent during the entire time they had been in Stormshock's grotto, finally spoke up. "Remember when we told you about the First Council rounding up all of the dangerous fey?" When Morgan nodded, he explained, "Hoarfrost Castle is where they were all locked away. It's further away than anywhere else, far enough that even if any of them escaped, there'd be nowhere for them to go."

Morgan remembered the story. Long ago, when the veil had first been erected, some of the fey didn't believe that the humans deserved magic and they wanted to make the barrier impenetrable so that only the fey had access to it. War broke out among the fey who wanted to keep the magic to themselves and those who wanted to share with the humans. Ultimately, the human-friendly side had won and those who continued to refuse that decision, such as the minotaur, were locked away. "So… this place is not so much of a castle," she mused. "It's more of a prison."

"That's exactly what it is," Askel agreed. "A prison that holds the fey who hate humans the most."

"What exactly am I being sent there for? Nobody actually told me what I am supposed to be doing once I get there."

"I can help with that," Vouivre explained as he joined them. "There are a few reasons for you to be sent there. First of all, the minotaur you encountered. They want confirmation on whether it escaped from Hoarfrost Castle or whether it was one that somehow evaded capture long ago."

"Why do *we* have to go find that out?" Tilson complained. "Couldn't someone else go instead?"

Ignoring the haltija's complaints, Vouivre continued his explanation. "The second reason is to determine whether any of the other prisoners have escaped or were released. That will give us an accurate idea of who and what we can expect to deal with."

"And by knowing whether any of the others are missing, that can help us determine whether there's someone on the outside helping them," Morgan realized. "Someone like Bas-Grann."

"Precisely. It is also hoped that by getting that information, we may uncover something that will lead to whatever is causing the petrification. If one of the fey are responsible for the attacks, by knowing who it is, we may be able to stop them and possibly even uncover a means by which we can undo the damage."

The weather had grown decidedly colder as they traveled and soon Morgan was glad that she had taken the precaution of putting on the ring that protected her against the cold. The landscape beneath them quickly turned from grass and trees with the occasional interruption of lakes and rivers, to a desolate white expanse. Signs of human life faded behind them, leaving only the snow to be seen in all directions. She pulled her sweatshirt tighter against herself, pulling her hands into the sleeves in order to keep them warm as well. One of these days, she mused to herself, she'd learn to keep a heavier coat in her satchel.

On the horizon, a faint shadow slowly came into view. As they approached, it grew larger and larger until Morgan could see it clearly, even at the distance from it they still were. A tall mountain soared upwards from the otherwise featureless white land, stretching even higher into the sky than Volcan's lair had. Ice and snow formations covered the side of the mountain but what drew Morgan's attention was what appeared to be the entrance of a building, formed entirely from crystal-clear ice. A pair of gargoyles hunched at the foot of the wide staircase that led to the opening, each of which appeared ready to strike. From what she had learned of her time in the fey, Morgan wouldn't be surprised if they did precisely that.

Askel and Vouivre landed a decent distance away from the base of the steps, far enough away that should the gargoyles attack, they would have enough time to react and defend themselves. Morgan slipped from the gryphon's back and caught Tilson as he dropped as well. Her feet sinking in snow almost up to her knees, she evaluated the entrance. "I guess there's not much question on where we need to go from here, is there?" She stuck the end of her staff into the ground, using its length to help her with balance on the treacherous surface.

Her eyes glanced from left to right into the expanse of snow, almost surprised that she didn't see Yukionna there. The snow maiden had almost captured Morgan the last time she had been in a frozen land such as this one, so it seemed like an appropriate time for a reunion. There was no sign of her, to Morgan's relief. Whether her absence was due to them not being in the same place at all or if it was because of Askel and Vouivre's presence, she didn't know.

Either way, she was relieved to have one less challenge to face.

Slowly and carefully, Morgan stepped toward the stairs, keeping a wary eye on the gargoyle sentinels as she approached. Slogging through the deep snow drifts was hard and she didn't want to even start thinking about how she would be able to fight off the fearsome beasts until the time came to actually react. The closer she got, however, the more surprised she became as the gargoyles remained motionless. "Are they here to keep us out?" she wondered, "or are they here to keep the prisoners in?"

Finally reaching the base of the stairs, she stepped to the side, reaching out a careful hand toward the closest one. When her hand encountered it, she was sure it would attack but there was no movement.

"They've been turned to stone," Tilson whimpered by her ear.

"Just like the ones back home," Morgan agreed. She hitched her satchel higher onto her shoulder, tucked the haltija into the hood of her sweatshirt in the hopes that he would be at least a little warmer there, readjusted her grip on her staff, and evaluated the stairs. With the gargoyles out of action, there was nothing to stop her from entering.

At least, nothing she could see.

With a resolved scowl, she began to climb.

16

STONEMAKER

The heavy ice doors didn't want to move but with Askel and Vouivre pushing, they swung inward with a loud, grating noise. "I guess they know we're here," Tilson grumbled but nobody paid him much attention.

Inside, Morgan was relieved to discover that the entire castle wasn't made out of ice, as it had appeared as they approached. While the first open space they encountered was covered in a thin, slippery sheet, she could see further inside that there was color, indicating that a substance more solid and less reflective lay beyond. They walked slowly and carefully across the treacherous surface, edging closer to what-ever lay beyond.

As they walked, the ice sheet thinned and soon they were able to detect signs of brown and gold tile beneath the frozen surface. The room narrowed until it was nothing more than a wide hall with stands placed at regular intervals along each side. Behind each stand, archways were cut into the wall and panels of smoky-grey glass covered the areas beyond each archway. The color and thickness of the glass made it hard to see what, if anything, lay beyond. Chandeliers, each dripping with a dizzying number of clear crystals, were suspended from the ceiling. Morgan stepped to the side of the hall to look more closely at one of the stands and the area beyond. Each stand, she discovered, had a piece of paper embedded in the top.

"What's a Borda Witch?" she asked.

"Borda Witch?" Tilson asked as he peered over her shoulder to see what she was looking at. "Never heard of one."

"I have," Askel stepped closer as well. "She's a sea witch, one of the most dangerous ones out there. Well, not a sea witch, I suppose, more of a swamp witch." He looked down at the page on the stand and then up at the glassy wall. "I guess she was one of those who opposed working with humans and was locked away in here. Strange, I would have expected her to be more in favor of the idea."

"Why?" Tilson asked.

"Because human is her favorite meal."

Morgan looked up at the gryphon, horrified. "She eats people?"

"It would appear she no longer does."

"So this is her prison cell?"

"I believe so, yes." He looked further down the hall. "Which would indicate that all of these glass panels are prison cells."

The hall extended well into the darkness, with silent cells looming on either side. Morgan shuddered slightly as she realized just how many of the fey had been locked away. Even though she knew there had been a lot, she hadn't expected to be this close to those who had been captured. The sheer quantity of cells she could see was staggering and the knowledge that there were more out of her range of view was almost overwhelming. "At least she's still locked away," she said as she examined the glass wall more closely. As far as she could tell, the wall was perfectly intact.

"I'm not so sure about that," Vouivre said as turned his ruby-colored eyes from the distant hall to the cell before them. "There's something different about some of these panels." He stepped forward, carefully leaning closer to the glass. When he was about a foot away, his eyes widened and he backed away. "There's nothing there!"

Morgan looked between the wall and the wyvern in confusion. "What do you mean, there's nothing there? Isn't there something in the cell?" If nothing else, she would have expected him to find the captured Borda Witch behind the smoky panel. "Did she escape?"

"Indeed," Vouivre answered. "Moreso, this wall you are examining does not exist."

She blinked a few times before turning back to the wall. "Doesn't exist? How can that be?"

"Oh!" Tilson hopped down from her shoulder and strode toward the wall. "I get it." Without meeting any resistance, he walked straight through the wall as though the glass wasn't even there. From the other side, he turned back to face his friends. "It's just an illusion."

Morgan's heart sank. If this wall was just an illusion, other cell walls could be illusory as well. Just how many of the incarcerated fey had managed to escape? "Okay," she said finally. "Let's spread out a little so we can make faster progress. If we touch a wall and it's real, we can assume that whatever is locked inside is still there. If it's just an illusion, we can assume it's gone. Sound reasonable?"

Everyone agreed so they began walking down the hallway, touching each of the walls in turn. While a handful of them remained solid, the vast majority we not real. As they discovered a missing captive, they read out what was on the stand, identifying the released fey. Most of them weren't creatures Morgan had previously heard of but some were just a little too familiar. "Minotaur," Tilson called out.

"And another over here," Askel added.

Eventually the hall ended in a T-shape, rows of cells that may or may not be occupied extending off to either side. "It would be faster for us to split up," Morgan began, "but all things considered, I'm not sure that's a good idea." If even a small amount of released fey were still in the building, she didn't want to face them alone. Nor did she want any of her friends to face them alone either. If the petrification attacks were caused by something that had once been locked away in this prison, she didn't want to lose another friend to it. A large part of her realized that had an escaped prisoner been the cause, there was little chance that they would return to the prison but she wasn't willing to risk it.

"I agree," Vouivre responded. "I am not comfortable separating from you in this place."

Morgan wasn't all that sure they needed to continue exploring Hoarfrost Castle, but she couldn't think of a good explanation for why she had stopped after only the first hall. On a whim, she selected the left-hand path and started down it, not surprised to see more empty chambers waiting. As far as she could tell, when she reported back to the High Council, the answer to how many of the fey had escaped would be "most of them." Only a few of the cells they had already checked were still occupied and she had no reason to believe they would discover anything different as they moved further into the forbidding building.

The few prisoners who were still present appeared to be frozen in time, silent and motionless. At first, she believed that they were actually frozen like the world outside but Askel corrected her when she asked about it. "They're under a stasis spell," he explained. "It's a type of magic that stops time for them. While many years have passed for all of us out here, none of them have been impacted by the intervening time."

"Isn't that bad, though?" she inquired. She couldn't help but draw a parallel between the captives under stasis and the spheres that had trapped the dragons' ether. "I mean, having all of the dragon ether trapped and taken out of circulation was what caused you guys to bring me in as a chosen in the first place. Seems like this is exactly the same thing. Doesn't locking away the ether of all these creatures have the same effect?"

"Yes and no," the gryphon explained. "First of all, the loss of the dragons was far more than just the loss of their ether. Dragons, as you may have already noticed, are not all that numerous among us. The loss of even a single dragon is a blow to all of feykind because they are so rare. When added to the fact that dragons live for a very long time, meaning that all of their knowledge and wisdom was lost alongside them, it becomes another factor. The idea that their ether was trapped and they could not be reborn was the final part of that issue."

Morgan nodded slowly, trying to comprehend what Askel was saying. While everything he explained was something she knew, on at least some level, there was still something about it that just felt wrong. "So these prisoners, since they and their ether are locked away, they can't die so they can't be reborn."

"That is correct. Should any of these prisoners die, their new form would be without blame. There would be no cause for them to be imprisoned, granting them another chance at restarting the war they once lost."

It wasn't all that different than the prison system they had in the human world, she supposed. As far as she understood it, when people did something that was so bad they needed to be locked away, they were taken to a prison similar to the one she currently stood in. While the humans weren't put under a stasis spell or anything like that, once the prisoner died, their crimes were effectively forgiven. "Do humans ever reincarnate too?" she wondered. "I mean, if fey go from one lifetime to another, does the same ever happen to a human?"

"You already know of one for whom that is true."

"The Mirror Man!" Tilson hopped up and down in excitement. "He's human, but he lives over and over like one of us. That means it is possible, right?"

The haltija was right. "Yeah, I guess so." Even so, she still wasn't sure she liked the idea of trapping all the fey who had been stored in the prison for as long as they had been held, even if they didn't realize how long they'd been there.

For now, the treatment of the prisoners was much lower on her list of priorities. She could bring her concerns to Stormshock and the rest of the High Council once she returned. For now, all she wanted to do was finish looking through the frigid building so they could leave.

"Stop." Vouivre held out a massive wing to keep the group from moving any further down the hallway. "I hear something ahead."

"I hear it as well," Askel agreed, "but I cannot see anything."

Morgan leaned forward, careful to stay behind the wyvern's protective wing, but couldn't hear or see anything. "What is it?"

"I cannot tell," Askel answered.

"Maybe we should just leave," Tilson offered. "We've mostly gotten what the council was asking for, so we really should go back and let them know what we've found out."

Although his argument closely echoed thoughts Morgan herself had only moments before, she wasn't as willing to leave quite yet. Certain that whatever lay ahead had to be one of the escaped prisoners, she looked nervously at her friends. "What do you guys think?"

"I think you should stay behind me," Vouivre answered. "Askel and I are here for your protection so it would not do for you to go running ahead of us."

Even though she didn't want to see anything happen to any of her friends, Morgan was willing to accept his suggestion. She stepped backwards, keeping some distance between herself and the two larger fey. Tilson, true to form, climbed up to her shoulder and promptly tucked himself into her hood.

Their decision made, the group began to move forward once again, no longer checking each of the prison cells as they passed. There didn't seem to be much of a point in continuing to check them, they were mostly empty anyway. Their reflections flashed as they moved and Morgan watched herself from the corner of her eye, wondering again whether the Mirror Man was watching over her. Her thoughts were derailed as she was finally able to detect the faint noises ahead, the sounds that had originally alerted Vouivre and Askel to the fact that they weren't alone. Shaking off her thoughts of Nathan and where he could be, she focused on the task at hand. If the source of the sounds was one of the escaped fey, she wasn't sure what she would do but she couldn't think of anything else that made sense to be there. It had to be one of the prisoners.

The hall ended in a room that was twice as

wide as the hall had been. The room was lit by a pair of flaming torches along each wall, eight in all. The torches burned brighter than Morgan would have expected until she discovered that they weren't torches at all. Instead, pots of oil were mounted to the walls. It was flames caused by these sconces of burning oil that caused the light. Their flickering glow danced across the room from the bare stone walls to the pair of broken pillars on the far side, up a short set of steps.

"Look," Morgan whispered. She pointed in the direction of one of the pillars, where the tail of a snake could be seen. "What is that?"

"Maybe it's the basilisk," Tilson offered. "You said that's what has been causing the petrification, right?"

Morgan nodded and moved closer. "You guys wait here," she said to Arien and Vouivre. "I'm going to get a closer look."

"Not a chance," Arien said as he blocked her movement with one of his wings. "You're not going ahead of us, we already decided that."

"Besides," Vouivre added, "we don't know

how to capture a basilisk yet. Even if we let you go ahead, what would you do?"

Morgan had to accept that they were right. Much as she wanted to move on the creature, she didn't have a plan.

"You may as well approach," a light feminine voice called out. "I know you're there. Why are you being so shy?"

Askel and Vouivre looked at Morgan in surprise, but she wasn't sure why they did so. When she asked, Askel pointed out, "She spoke to us."

"I know. I heard." She indicated her amulet, which translated everything into a language she could understand.

"She spoke to us in your language," Vouivre added. "Your amulet did not translate that."

She blinked for a moment as the meaning behind his words sank in. "I don't suppose basilisks speak in a human language, do they?" Askel shook his head, so she craned her neck to see past him, wondering what else waited for them. In her opinion, the basilisk alone would be more than enough.

Before she could question further, a woman

appeared from the other side of the column. At least, Morgan initially believed it to be a woman but her body ended in the tail of a snake, like a twisted mermaid that had somehow made its way onto land. The woman's hair writhed around her face with unseen wind and Vouivre sucked in his breath sharply.

"Gorgon."

Morgan didn't recognize the word, which was no surprise. Yet again, the fey called themselves by different names than those known to humans. The creature's appearance, however, made what she was obvious.

"It's a medusa," she breathed.

"Not quite," the gorgon said, sliding closer as she spoke. "Medusa was my sister, killed long ago. My name is Eurale."

Scales grew down onto her face, framing it in a strange shimmer. Beneath the framing scales, her eyes were almost too human in appearance, bright green, the color of emeralds. Her skin was tinted green, lighter than the snakes that grew from her head but not by much. The color darkened once again as it reached her tail, spotted only by the occasional yellow patch. She wore no clothing, the only adornment on her body other than her jewel-colored scales was a golden necklace at her throat.

Tilson shrieked at her words and jumped to the floor, heading back in the direction from which they had come, his tail sticking straight out behind him as he ran.

Eurale moved with lightning speed, every bit as quick and nimble as the snakes that formed parts of her body. Before Morgan registered the movement, the gorgon was behind them, blocking their exit. "Why so rude?" Eurale asked. "I have introduced myself; you should do the same."

"Do not look at her," Vouivre hissed. "Those who meet her eyes fall victim to her power."

Morgan didn't need to be told. Stories about Medusa, the fearsome snake-woman in some of the most ancient stories still repeated in her world, were well-known indeed. She understood immediately that to meet the woman's eyes would only result in her own petrification, but she found her voice strangely appealing. She immediately looked downward, squeezing her eyes closed in an attempt to not become a statue herself.

"You..." she stammered, "you're supposed to be locked away in one of these cells."

"I was," Eurale purred. "I was only released a few months ago."

"So why are you doing all this now?" Morgan had to know.

"Imagine my surprise when I found out just how long I'd been in stasis. When we were locked away, it was only supposed to have been for a short period of time so that the veil could be erected. Not only were we not released as promised when the veil was complete but it was a human, of all things, who released me."

"A human?" Morgan almost looked up in surprise at the gorgon's words but she caught herself just in time. "What human?"

"Who he was is of little concern to you. All you need to know is that in return for my freedom, I have agreed to follow the orders of my new Meister."

Morgan's knees threatened to buckle entirely at this latest revelation. There was only one person who Eurale could be referring to.

Only one person Morgan had ever heard refer to himself as a Meister. "Ameil Bas-Grann." It seemed as though every direction she turned, all she saw were those who worked for the horrid man.

"Ah, so you know of him. That makes things easier."

Even as the thoughts washed over her and she tried to regain her balance, Morgan's fingers fumbled in her pockets, searching for anything that could help. She didn't dare open her eyes for fear of accidentally catching a glimpse of Eurale's dangerous eyes. Deciding she had nothing of use in her pockets, she turned her attention to her satchel.

"We need to leave this place," Askel said, his voice reflecting every bit as much fear as Morgan herself felt. "We have no means of defeating her here."

"When I say so," Vouivre spoke up, "run for the exit. As fast as you can and do not look behind you."

Again Morgan had to resist the urge to look up at her friends. "What are you going to do?" she whispered back.

She could practically feel the reassuring smile in his voice as he answered. "Do not worry about me. I will catch up with you outside."

Listening all the while for the telltale sounds of Eurale's movements, Morgan risked cracking an eye to scan the floor. She turned slightly, angling herself toward the hallway from which they had come.

"Now!" Vouivre's voice thundered through the room, propelling Morgan to run. Just inside the doorway, she scooped up Tilson's tiny form, cradling him in her arms as she ran. Clattering sounds behind her, the unmistakable sound of Askel's claws, indicated that the gryphon was not too far behind. An unholy shriek echoed Vouivre's call before she had gotten more than five steps into the hallway. Biting back tears of fear and anger, Morgan ran for all she was worth for the exit, praying that her friends stayed safe and that everyone would reach safety together. Smoked glass walls and paper-inlaid columns flew past as she ran.

Her feet shot out from beneath her when she hit the icy section of floor, causing her to slide forward at almost the same rate of speed she had been maintaining as she ran but without nearly as much control. Shrieking in surprise and barely keeping hold of Tilson, she barely managed to readjust her center of balance and pull her feet back underneath her before tumbling onto the slippery surface. She stayed low in a crouch, trying to maintain what little balance she could muster, as she slid out through the door and down the steps that lay beyond, both arms wrapped carefully around the haltija for his safety. Her momentum slowed when she reached the snow-covered ground and she shot to her feet, resuming her panicked dash away from the building.

She screamed in fresh terror when she was hoisted into the air, strong talon-tipped claws wrapping carefully around her to lift her from the ground. Her screaming stopped only a moment later when she recognized the claw as belonging to Askel. Unlike the last time he had caught her while she was moving, this time his claws didn't dig into her flesh. They coiled around her like iron bands, capturing her completely and ensuring she wouldn't fall.

The gryphon lifted her higher into the air

before letting go, dropping her onto Vouivre's leathery back. Only then did Morgan look around, pleased that both Arien and Vouivre had made it out alive but fearful of what they had left behind. "What happened back there?" she asked once she got her voice back under control. "Why did you say we couldn't defeat her?"

"Eurale is an Ancient," Vouivre answered. "She cannot be defeated by normal methods. I believe you have some experience in such matters."

She did. If Eurale truly was an Ancient as the wyvern said, that made the challenge much more difficult. The last Ancient who had targeted Morgan had almost killed her before she figured out how to defeat it.

She turned her attention to the tiny form in her arms. Tilson hadn't moved at all during the flight from Hoarfrost Castle. Normally that would have been surprising, considering how often the haltija complained about everything Morgan did, particularly when she handled him roughly. Her tears flowed freely as she cradled his tiny body. This time, the stone figure would be offering no complaints.

17

FEY IN THE HUMAN WORLD

Morgan didn't sleep on the journey home from Hoarfrost Castle. A couple times, Askel and Vouivre tried to engage her in conversation but she refused to speak. Her mind was filled, cluttered with an ever-increasing cycle of thoughts and feelings, none of which was she in any mood to deal with rationally.

When the petrification attacks had first started, she had been irritated but they hadn't directly impacted her. Sure, having people and fey being turned to stone was definitely a bad thing but despite her position as a chosen it hadn't felt personal. It hadn't started to feel personal to her until Tellius was attacked. When the attack upon Zea Island occurred, it became very, very personal. Not only were those her friends, now turned into stone statues, she herself had been present for the attack. That was the part that bothered her the most. She had been there; she had been asleep. She alone had been saved while everyone around her had been turned to stone. And she still had no idea how or why.

That loss had hurt, certainly, but it was nothing compared to losing Tilson. He had been the first fey she had met, her best friend since she had moved to Denver Heights. Despite his constant complaints and their frequent arguments, he had always been there for her, her companion on all of her adventures working with the fey. Even the one time he had decided it was too dangerous for him to continue joining in her adventures, he had still been there for her when she needed him the most. Now, when he had needed her the most, she hadn't been able to save him. Again, she had been right there and yet unable to do anything about it.

"We will take him with us," Askel said as they arrived at Morgan's house. "We can keep him safe with the others until a restorative is found."

"No." The first word Morgan had spoken since leaving Hoarfrost Castle left no room for argument. "He stays with me." Without waiting for further argument, she carried the precious statue inside and up the stairs.

Apparently having already been apprised of the situation, Liore watched helplessly as Morgan placed Tilson onto a shelf. "Are you okay?" the elvor finally asked. "Vouivre told us about what happened," she explained gently.

Morgan shook her head. "No. No, I'm not okay. How could I possibly be okay with everything that's happening?" Her voice rose as she spoke, revealing her emotional state quite clearly. "It's another Ancient," she explained, lowering her voice to more normal levels. "It wasn't a basilisk after all. And this time, I don't even have the Mirror Man to help me find a way to stop her."

"You're not alone," Liore reminded her. "We all want this to end, just as badly as you do." She wrapped her arms around Morgan and hugged her. "There's got to be a way to stop her."

She was right, Morgan already understood that if Eurale had been locked away once, she could be locked away again. Maybe Morgan wouldn't be able to kill her as she had done with the Djieien but even if she was just locked back in her cell, or somewhere else where she wouldn't be able to hurt anyone ever again, it would stop her rampage.

"She's working with Ameil Bas-Grann," she explained as she wiped tears from her face. "He just keeps sending more and more after me." At first it had only been deception and subterfuge that confronted her but the longer Ameil remained at large, the more direct his threats became. And the more dangerous. "First he attacked the dragons, then he spread that sickness that we needed the cuélebre for. After that was the Djieien and I barely survived that one. Now he's sent Eurale and I have no clue how to stop her yet." Determination shone in her eyes as she looked at her friend. "Or him. If he's not stopped soon, who knows what he'll do next or how much damage he'll cause."

Liore stayed with her until Morgan calmed. Once she was sure that she would be okay, she caught her up on what had been happening while Morgan had been at Hoarfrost Castle. "As I understand it, the High Council has ordered you to be under constant guard, so either he or Askel will be here all the time. I'll drop by when I can, too."

"That's probably not necessary," Morgan said, "but I appreciate it anyway."

Liore grinned at her, humor dancing behind her eyes as she did. "Even if they hadn't ordered it, I'm sure you'd have plenty of us watching over you. After all, he's come after you directly once, so there's no reason to think he won't try again." She continued to explain that almost all of feykind was in an uproar, each of the individual councils reporting one level of panic or another.

"Seems like Ameil's plan to drop the veil is creeping closer to success," she pointed out. "And there's another thing you should be aware of. Remember Brittany?"

How could Morgan forget? The vile girl and her friends had been tormenting Liore to the extent that Corran had pulled her from the human world entirely. In fact, now that she had a clearer head to think about it, Morgan was surprised that Liore had been allowed to return as Morgan's stand-in while she was out.

"Oh, I wasn't sent here," Liore waved off her question. "I'm still supposed to be safe and sound at home. But I couldn't just leave your place undefended, so when I heard you were being sent out again, I came on my own."

"You're allowed to do that?"

"Not exactly but I don't think anyone is in much of a mood to stop me right now." She flashed her trademark grin once more before sobering. "But those girls, I think they have something to do with Ameil."

Morgan blinked at her a couple times, her mouth falling slightly open in surprise. "I..." she stammered, "I kinda already knew that."

"You knew?"

"Yeah," Morgan shrugged one shoulder. "I mean, maybe I didn't know but I suspected. They never said as much but a lot of the things they said made it seem like they were working with him for some reason." She flopped onto her bed. "I still don't see why he would be work-ing with them, though. The whole thing just doesn't make much sense." She flung an arm over her eyes, as though to block out whatever would be coming at her next. "What did they do now?"

"She's still making her catty comments all the time, pretty much every chance she gets, really, but they seem to be a lot more specific to what's going on than I would have expected. She's made a lot of references to statues and other things that wouldn't be normal for high-school girls to talk about."

Morgan couldn't think of a single time in either her current school or her previous one where statues had been a topic of conversation, so she agreed that it seemed odd for Brittany and her friends to talk about them now. "What else has she mentioned?"

"She asked me if I had any thoughts on what happened to fairies after they die."

Morgan froze and looked over at the elvor, certain that she must have misheard somehow. "She did what? Did she really specifically say fairies?"

Liore nodded. "Like I said, super weird stuff, right? I mean, she called them by the wrong name, but it was pretty obvious she was talking about peri."

This wasn't something Morgan had considered. She knew that Brittany and her little group were a personal thorn in her backside, Liore's as well, but even when she included the snide comments the trio had made before, she hadn't expected to find anything that would directly lead her to believe they were connected to the fey. Even the comments about statues could have been just a coincidence, much as she didn't want to believe it. Morgan's suspicions that they were connected to Ameil had been based on nothing substantial, but now she had to put a bit more thought into the idea. Maybe a lot more. It was all just becoming too obvious, too many comments to be accidental. A fresh chill ran down her spine as one potential explanation became apparent. "Do you think one of them might be a chosen?"

Liore shook her head. "Nope. I had the same thought, so I checked on that first thing. None of the councils have any knowledge of any of them. If there's a chosen in that group, particularly since there's already a chosen here, we'd have known about it already."

"Why would they work with someone like Ameil?" Morgan wondered. "Or, from the other side, why would someone like Ameil work with a bunch of annoying teenagers like them?" She couldn't imagine any way in which the obnoxious girls could help with the so-called Meister's agenda.

The elvor cocked her head and looked askance at Morgan. "One thought comes to mind," she said pointedly. "Like you said earlier, Ameil's been targeting you from pretty much every direction he's been able to target you from. Each time, you've been able to slip through his fingers and avoid all of his traps. Maybe he's trying to get at you from the human world now, too."

"Not all of his traps. I've fallen into a fair share of them." Morgan didn't like the idea but she couldn't dispute the logic. His most successful attacks against her had all been while she had been at home. "But why teenagers?

Wouldn't it have made more sense to come after my parents or something like that?"

Liore shook her head again. "Your dad was a chosen, remember? That automatically means that he's got more defenses than the average person, even if he doesn't remember any of it. Plus, you have to understand that kids are usually a lot more susceptible to manipulation than adults are."

"If he's just manipulating them, do you think they'll calm down once he's been stopped?"

"That would be my guess. If he's promised them something, they'll probably turn their backs on him when he doesn't deliver."

Her words struck a mental chord with Morgan. "That's it!" she exclaimed. "He promised them things."

Now it was Liore's turn to look confused. "What do you mean?"

"Something they said to me a while ago, they're all supposed to be rich and famous in a handful of ways. I think one was supposed to be a model and another was supposed to be a rock star or something like that."

Liore nodded slowly. "That would make a lot

of sense. At least, those all sound like things that they'd be interested in getting out of the deal." She smiled without any actual humor behind it. "Not that I have any clue why all of you humans are so obsessed with being famous. So all you have to do is make sure he can't give them what they want, and they'll probably calm down on their own." She chuckled. "They might even turn on him and end up being an asset instead of such a hindrance."

An idea was beginning to form in Morgan's mind but she wasn't quite ready to share it with the elvor yet. She needed more time to figure out how to do it. "Any word from any of the other councils on how to undo the petrification?"

"Nothing yet. Cristin got called back in by the High Council to pick up where Arien stopped. He's still getting caught up with what Arien had in his notes but hopefully he'll come up with something soon."

Cristin was an apotharni, just like Arien but with darker fur and hair. He worked with a different council but had been called to work with the fey on Zea Island once before. Morgan hadn't been able to spend much time with him while he was there previously but he seemed like he knew what he was doing. At least, Arien thought he did. She was willing to trust Arien's judgment on that.

Thoughts of Arien threatened to spiral Morgan back into her depression but she shook them away. She didn't have time to deal with that right now.

"Oh, one other thing," Liore said as she perched on the window sill, preparing to leave. "Your magic. You can practice here if you want, nobody's going to come stop you, but the council has decided that it's too dangerous to send anyone out to train you right now." Her face twisted up at the words.

"Let me guess," Morgan said, "Corran?"

"You got it."

It wasn't much of a guess. Corran had been against Morgan being taught magic from the very beginning. Morgan had long wondered what his hesitation about it was but he had been firm in his decision. It hadn't been until Magicgleam had overridden his decision that she had begun to learn even the most rudimentary parts of spellcasting. Almost the entire time she had spent working with the fey as their chosen, Morgan had done so without the aid of magic, or at least without the aid of spells. She had plenty of magical items to help her, others had seen to that as well. She had only recently gotten her hands on an honest-to-goodness spell book and even that hadn't been easy. She had found it, or rather Tilson had found it, buried underneath a pyramid in Egypt on one of her trips there. Because she was so used to working without spells, she hardly ever thought about the book until she needed something from it.

After Liore left, ducking out the window as all of the fey seemed to do, Morgan flopped on her bed to decide what to do next. Maybe the spell book that Liore had referenced would have something useful in it, she supposed. Now that she was able to read the magical language, at least at a basic level, she might be able to uncover something useful.

"At least I can read these now," she muttered to herself. The first time she had cast a spell, she had required Askel's assistance. The gryphon had read the words on each page as Morgan flipped through the book and then had needed to pronounce everything for her to repeat and cast. At the time, she had wondered whether it had even been her who cast the spell but Askel had assured her that it had been her magic and not his to release the Ghirtablili.

For the next week, she spent most of her time at home in her bedroom, looking through the book and her assortment of notes, searching for a solution. She barely touched her homework but made sure she did enough to get by. Thankfully, Liore had continued to make extensive notes on what happened in class so Morgan was able to understand what needed to be done.

Sometimes she would take a break from her studies, both magical and mundane, to look up at Tilson where he waited on her shelf. Not that she needed the encouragement to keep going, as she knew full well what was relying on her. The weight of the responsibility she carried was heavy but there was no other choice. She simply wished she had a solution already. Even if he did complain more than anything else, she wished her friend was back to normal for her to talk with. Missing him while he was gone was one thing but missing him while he was standing in front of her was completely different and so much worse.

Just as Liore had said they would, either Askel or Vouivre stayed close at hand. One or the other of them was constantly nearby, most often at the edge of her yard where the treeline started. So far, Morgan hadn't seen anything that would warrant their continued presence but that didn't mean there hadn't been any threats yet. For all she knew, the fey were simply handling things as they came up and then going back to monitoring the situation without telling her anything. It did strike her as strange that she had somehow become one of the people who had guardians. Until now, the only ones who had guards assigned to them had been the Ancients. Since she was supposed to be the one guarding the fey, rather than the other way around, it struck her as odd. It wasn't even like she was doing a good job of taking care of them.

Despite her doubts about her own performance, one thing she was absolutely sure about was that more of the fey were beginning to act up in the human world. What had first started as a handful of mischievous fey causing problems for the humans had increased in both frequency and in danger. Some of these had resulted in the fire that had been set at her school, damage from which had only recently been repaired, and the theft of stop signs that had resulted in multiple accidents, a few of which had turned out to be fatal. Humans coming into contact with the fey were starting to notice and Morgan wasn't sure whether or not that was a good thing. Most of the encounters that she heard of were with creatures about which Morgan already knew, creatures such as the peri or gremlins. Others reported encounters with creatures Morgan hadn't even heard of. Worse, not all of the encounters were with creatures actively trying to cause problems, many of them were just random sightings of fey who weren't trying to be seen.

None of these encounters should have happened. The glamour that kept the worlds of the humans and the fey separated should have prohibited any of the humans from seeing the fey among them. "Does this mean that the veil is thinning?" she wondered. "Is that even a thing?" She had assumed that there were thicker and thinner parts of the veil, but for the first time she questioned whether that was correct. "Maybe it's just an on or off thing, where either it's there or it's not."

One night, while seated at the kitchen table and finishing up a particularly tricky set of homework problems while waiting for dinner to be ready, she overheard her parents discussing the latest series of events. More vandalism had been on the news, reports that spanned into the neighboring towns that had been attributed to gang activity, even though most of the witnesses reported strange creatures in the vicinity.

"I thought smaller towns were supposed to be safer. That's why we chose this area in the first place." her mother said, "If there are gangs here, maybe moving here wasn't as good of an idea after all. It doesn't seem to be much safer than the town we were at before at all."

"Looks that way," her father sighed. "But I haven't been at my job for very long, so I can't exactly ask for a transfer already. And it's really not as bad here as it was back there, it just seems worse because that's all everyone's talking about lately. When there's not much news to be had, all of the news sounds much more important."

"Wouldn't hurt to talk to them about it, at the very least." Susan Lafayette worked from home, so it didn't matter where they lived. As long as they had internet service, she had a stable job. David, Morgan's father, was a different story. He worked in a bank and that required him to be in the office to do his work.

"There are other branches you can talk to," she continued. "I'm sure one of them somewhere needs someone new in your position." She turned the television off and headed for the kitchen to stir the pot of bubbling spaghetti sauce. "Pretty much anywhere seems like it would be safer than here right now."

"We can't move," Morgan spoke up. While she understood her parents' concern, she couldn't risk moving and having all of the activity follow her to their new home. "I have school still. The year just started. It's not fair to pull me out again like this."

"She has a point," David agreed from the doorway. "We just had her transferred here and she's only just started to make friends. You can't just pull her out and have her start all over again."

"Well then, what do you suggest we do?" Susan glared at her husband. She wasn't really mad, but her concerns were valid.

"We get a security system," David said. "And if we still need to move after Morgan graduates, we can look at it again then."

~ 18 ~

RETURN TO CEARA TEMPLE

"We have received word from Magicgleam." The voice came from a white-winged peri as she fluttered in through Morgan's open bedroom window.

"Let me guess," Morgan responded irritably. "They still don't have a cure, nobody knows how to stop Eurale or Ameil, and I get to continue waiting here indefinitely."

"Well, aren't we the grouchy one today?"

"Sorry," Morgan looked up from her notebook to meet the peri's eyes. "This has been a really tough week for me."

"For all of us," the peri agreed in a much softer voice. "But your guess is incorrect. The message from Magicgleam says that you are to go immediately to Ceara Temple. Nitsa is waiting there for you."

"Ceara Temple? Why am I being sent there?"

"I do not know. I just know that this came from Magicgleam and that everything will be explained once you arrive."

Morgan sighed and began putting away her things. She glanced over at the statue of Tilson, wondering whether he would be safe there while she was gone. Perhaps it would have been better had she let Askel take him to keep with the rest of the petrified fey but she couldn't bear to let him go like that.

"He will be safe in your absence," the peri explained gently. "Attacks upon your home are rare while you are away and Liore will be here to keep an eye on things as well."

"Shouldn't she be here by now, then? How is she going to keep an eye on things if she's not even here?"

"She has another matter that she needs to

resolve before coming here. I will remain until her arrival."

Morgan blinked at the peri doubtfully. As with all of the peri, the tiny girl was less than six inches in height. While she had the same ability to fly as did all the peri, Morgan wasn't sure how effective she would be in defending anything, should her home come under attack. "I don't see how much good that will do," she said finally. "If Ameil sends something here, how could you possibly do anything about it?"

"You must be joking," the peri responded. She crossed her arms, hovering in the air in front of Morgan's face, her own brows furled in affront. "You do realize that we peri have some of the most powerful magic of all the fey, do you not?"

"I..." Morgan stammered. "I didn't know that. I've never seen any of you do much at all."

The peri sighed and settled down onto the desk with one last indignant flick of her wings. "When it comes to pure magical power, the only ones with more of it are the dragons. But it wouldn't actually do to have one of them safe-guarding your home, as they are far too large and there are too few of them available. But we peri have remained almost entirely unscathed throughout this entire ordeal."

"How?" Morgan was shocked at the idea. She had no idea that the tiny creatures were so powerful, almost strong enough to rival a dragon. As she thought about it, however, she realized that although many of the other fey had fallen to one or another of Ameil's traps, the peri had always managed to make it through without taking much damage at all. Of those who had been petrified lately, only one or two had been peri, which she should have been more surprised to note. She had just assumed that was due to the sheer number of the peri available. Her father even had a term he used for it, strength in numbers, or something like that. The idea that the diminutive fey could be so powerful in their own right, as individuals rather than just in groups, hadn't even crossed her mind.

"Really. What have they been teaching you?" the peri grumbled. "Regardless, you have no time for this now. You need to go to meet up with Nitsa in her temple. She awaits."

"Right, right." Morgan stood and stretched before heading to retrieve her supplies from the closet. In preparation for just such a call, she had packed her satchel with everything she thought she would, or even might, need. Too many times, she had wished to have one or more of her magical items, only to realize when it was too late that the item she needed was still tucked away safely at home. She made a quick check of the contents, specifically ensuring that the arm cuff that allowed her to breathe water was still there. Satisfied, she turned and looked back at the peri.

"Okay, I guess I'm off, then."

The peri waved her off and Morgan put on her cloak before heading for the stairs. She didn't want to run the risk of having her mother see her as she was leaving, as there wasn't any good way to explain where she was going. Not that it mattered, of course. Her mother was in her office with the door closed, engaged in one of her phone call meetings, just as she was almost every afternoon. If she even noticed her daughter creeping down the hall, she made no indication of it. Not that she would have, of course, as the combination of closed door and Morgan's Cloak of Concealment ensured she wouldn't be spotted.

Just beyond the front door, Askel waited patiently for her. Wearing the cloak, she was invisible to even the gryphon's keen eyesight but even so she had never been able to sneak up on him. He lowered himself to the ground to let her climb onto his back and get settled before taking flight.

Once they were airborne, she removed the cloak and tucked it back into her satchel. There was no worry about her being seen, by her parents or anyone else, while they flew so there was no reason to wear the cloak. "Been a while since I've been to Ceara Temple," she said. "Do you know why I'm being sent there again?"

"I do not," the gryphon responded as he ascended until he was just beneath the layer of clouds. "But I am pleased to see that you are in better spirits today."

"Am I?" As far as Morgan could tell, she was still feeling grouchy. Even the messenger peri had made a comment about it.

"Indeed," he chuckled. "You are even speaking once more."

They chatted light-heartedly, neither of them wanting to bring up anything that would cause yet another strain in the conversation, throughout the journey to the ocean. They landed in a grassy area just outside the water, where the grass met sand before becoming ocean.

Resting on the sandy shore, just as it had been previously, waited a simple wooden boat with no oars. The first time Morgan had taken the boat to the temple, she had been confused on the absence of oars and sails, uncertain about how she would get to the underwater temple, but the boat had delivered her to and from the temple safely, just as she had been promised. This time, she had no such hesitation and settled into the boat without complaint or question. She waved to Askel as the boat slipped out to the water, watching as her friend faded from view.

Once she could no longer see the shore, she dug in her satchel to retrieve the armband she had been given the first time she had made the journey. It was a lot sturdier than it looked, formed of a series of carved seashells, and she had little concern about its effectiveness. She started to slip it over her wrist before remembering why that was a bad idea. While she was underwater, it allowed her to breathe as freely as she could above the surface but when she was above the waves and in the open air, it caused her to choke as though air was no longer breathable.

She lost track of time as she bobbed across the waves, watching as a massive school of fish swam past beneath her, glinting silver and white in the reflected sun, and laughing with amusement at a group of grey-skinned and pointy-nosed dolphins who appeared after the school of fish. The dolphins leaped and danced through the water, diving through the waves. They chatted amongst each other as they played, confirming to Morgan's ears that they were just having fun. "Apparently humans aren't the only ones who like playing in the water," she mused. She looked on in awe as a massive shadow appeared below her, slowly rising to the surface until it just broke through into open air. The whale sprayed water high into the air before dropping down to become a shadow once more. Briefly, she considered slipping on the armband and ducking her head into the water to speak to the enormous creature but she decided against it. Had it been feeling chatty, she would have heard it already.

Eventually even the dolphins disappeared behind her and the whale's shadow disappeared into the gloom and Morgan was left on her own again, raising a hand to shield against the glare of the setting sun as she looked out at the endless expanse of water. This far out to sea, even the birds had long since disappeared. Finally, the boat appeared to slow in its journey, indicating that they had arrived. She stood and slipped her satchel over her shoulder, picking up her staff and looking around, waiting to see who would appear. She rotated the shell bracelet in her hand nervously, running her thumb over each of the shells in turn like a string of strange rosary beads while she waited.

Bubbles formed in the water next to the boat, quickly growing into a geyser of water. The geyser, nowhere near as tall as that made by the whale, quickly formed into a familiar figure.

Blue-grey skin covered the human shape from waist up, beneath that was nothing more than water. Fan-shaped ears jutted out of the figure's head and Morgan grinned as she recognized the naiad. "Laasya. Good to see you again."

"And you as well, chosen. Are you ready to begin?"

"I am." Even as she spoke, she took a deep breath and slipped the shell band onto her arm. Without needing any prompting, she dove into the water, holding out one hand for Laasya to grasp.

As she had done the last time, Laasya took Morgan's warm hand in her own cold one and pulled her down beneath the water. The water temperature dropped the further they went but didn't quite become cold enough to be problematic. Vision narrowed as the water blocked out more and more of the light, but Morgan wasn't concerned. Her companion knew where they were headed. Five minutes later, she spotted the familiar lights of the temple twinkling in the distance.

Ceara Temple was an enormous building on the floor of the ocean, made of stone and covered with sediment and sea plants. Archways bloomed out of the central building like the petals of a massive flower. It was toward one of these archways that the naiad brought Morgan. The bright flowers and vines that she remembered from her previous visit were still present but sadly none appeared to be in bloom. Also unlike her last visit, the swarms of merfolk she had spotted before were nowhere to be seen. The entire place seemed quiet and subdued, vacant but for Morgan and the naiad.

The archway led into an area that was illuminated with a yellow-orange light. Inside the room, Nitsa waited for her. "Greetings once again, chosen, and thank you for coming. I trust you have been well."

"I suppose so." Morgan pursed her lips. All things considered, she wouldn't consider herself to have been well but she hadn't been turned to stone, so that was something. She refrained from saying as much to Nitsa, however, as the mermaid hadn't done anything wrong by asking. It wouldn't be fair to have come all this way just to start an argument, after all.

As though understanding her thoughts,

Nitsa's friendly smile softened. "I know this must be a very difficult time for you, so I will be directly to the point. I believe we know of something that may assist you."

Morgan nodded quietly and followed her as she headed deeper into the temple. This was hardly the first time that the fey of Ceara Temple had given her important information, so she had already half-expected the mermaid's statement.

"We had initially hoped to bring you here," Nitsa explained as they went, "to help you in your magical training. Magicgleam informed us that your current tutor is not available and that you lacked a suitable place to learn from trained spellcasters where you would not be interrupted. Given our latest discovery, we have decided that information is more important than training for you to have at this time."

"What kind of information?" Morgan hadn't expected that the possibly of learning how to cast magic from merfolk would have been an option and was a little disappointed that it now sounded like that wouldn't happen. Yet again, her ability to learn magic had been hindered.

She was starting to wonder if she would ever become a full-fledged magic user.

"The gorgon you encountered, Eurale. She is an Ancient."

"Yeah, that's what Askel and Vouivre told me too. As far as I know, all of the Ancients have a special way they can be stopped or killed but I have no idea how to stop her."

"And that is why you have been brought here." The mermaid looked over her shoulder and smiled again at her. "Moreso, the means by which you may do so may be easier than any of us could have expected."

"Easier?" Morgan raised an eyebrow at the word. "She turns people to stone. How could that be considered easier?"

"Because she carries her heart with her."

Morgan had heard a similar term before, when she had sought a way to defeat the Djieien. At first, she had been confused when she had been told that he, like many of the Ancients, carried his heart outside of his body. That confusion had cleared up when she discovered that his heart was actually the heart of his power. It had only been by finding and destroying his heart that she had finally been safe from the massive spider. "So she has one of those heart things too?" Perhaps, she realized, had she still possessed the Cup of Jamshid, she could have used that to locate her heart as she had done before, this whole thing could have been over already. But that was out of the question, as she had turned it over to Stormshock and it had likely already been returned to Fantas. Without the Mirror Man's assistance, it was completely out of her reach now.

"Indeed. And that is why you are here." She stopped in front of the same storage room Morgan had been brought to previously, when the amplifier was stolen. The same amplifier, in fact, that was still attached to her arm.

From what Morgan remembered, the room Nitsa stopped at was used to store dangerous items, those believed to be too hazardous to store on the surface above. As she watched, Nitsa went inside and rummaged for a moment before coming back out with a scroll.

"This describes an artifact known as the Necklace of Harmonia," the mermaid explained. "From the descriptions we were given, it sounds as though Eurale was wearing it when you encountered her."

Curious, Morgan broke the wax seal and unrolled the parchment. Just as with the last scroll she had been given by the residents of Ceara Temple, this one didn't seem to be affected by the water. The first thing she noted was a careful sketch that perfectly depicted the golden necklace the gorgon had worn. It was beautifully formed in the shape of two snakes of some variety whose mouths formed the clasp. Small gemstones were set into the snakes' bodies, two of the largest of which formed the eyes of each serpent. "That's it!" she exclaimed as she looked back up into Nitsa's face. Although she hadn't noticed the jewels in the snakes, she was absolutely certain it was the same jewelry. "Will this necklace help to stop her?"

"Quite the opposite. We believe that this necklace is the source of her power. Her heart."

Morgan turned back to the scroll with deepened interest and unrolled it further. "The Necklace of Harmonia," she read, "allows any woman wearing it to remain eternally young and beautiful." She looked back up in shock at what she read. "This works for anyone? Not just Eurale?"

"It seems that way. I have never seen the Necklace of Harmonia myself but from what legends I have heard, any woman who dons that necklace will remain precisely as they are until the necklace is removed."

Morgan continued scanning the scroll, where she discovered that the necklace was once known to humans. "Where is Thebes?" she wondered. She made a mental note to look it up later, once she was back above water. There was no reason to expect the mermaid to have any clue where Thebes was. "So if I manage to take this necklace away from her, she becomes mortal again?" The idea made sense. If what the scroll said was true, it was no wonder that Askel and Vouivre had insisted they not stay and fight. While Eurale wore the Necklace of Harmonia, she was practically invincible. Only, minus the 'practically' part. This necklace meant that she couldn't be killed at all. So how was she supposed to get the necklace away from the gorgon without being turned into a statue in the process?

"That is the assumption we came to and the rest of the High Council has agreed that it is the most logical solution. From what we were able to uncover, it was by removing this necklace that Eurale was imprisoned to begin with."

"So how did she get it back?" Morgan wondered. "Was it stolen from here too?"

"No," Nitsa shook her head. "We were not the keepers of this artifact and I know not where it was held."

She wanted to ask so many more questions, not just about the necklace but also about Eurale herself, the High Council, any tips the mermaid may have had on learning magic, and what had happened to the rest of the merfolk, but a commotion interrupted them before Morgan was able to ask anything.

"We have found you, little one." A tall, slender woman strode into the corridor. She had deep green skin and bluish-black veining all over, blood-red lips and black fingertips. Animal bodies, fish, octopuses, and even what appeared to be a very small shark, each of which were obviously no longer alive, were wrapped around her body like macabre armor. "Did you think yourself safe down here?"

Even in the cold water, the sight of the strange woman sent a chill down Morgan's spine. She recognized the woman from a picture she had seen not long ago, while she had been investigating Hoarfrost Castle. "It's the Borda Witch," she breathed. "What's she doing here?"

"Run," Nitsa maneuvered to position herself between Morgan and the Borda Witch. "She has too much power down here. Get back to the surface where it is safe."

As the mermaid and the witch squared off, Morgan looked around, trying to see what she could do to help. She was a chosen, after all, tasked with protecting and assisting the fey. Nitsa was not only a fey but her friend and the appearance of the Borda Witch could only mean that the mermaid was in danger.

With a flick of her tail, Nitsa thrust a wall of water in her direction. The pressure sent Morgan shooting backwards, through another open doorway. "Laasya will join you shortly. Start heading for the surface!"

Afraid of what would happen to the temple

guardian when she left but knowing there was little she could do to assist, Morgan began to swim. She headed for the first opening in the ceiling she came to, immediately finding herself out in open water. The depths made it impossible to see much beyond the meager glow of the temple, which soon faded behind her as she headed upwards.

She wasn't the strongest swimmer but at least she knew the basics. Bodies naturally tried to float up to the surface, so anytime she started to lose her direction, or to even question which way she needed to be heading, she simply stopped moving to see which direction she naturally moved. Much as she hoped that Nitsa would be a match for the witch, the sinking feeling in her stomach told her otherwise. The witch was dangerous enough to have been locked away in Hoarfrost Castle, so she would likely be more than a match for Nitsa. She knew there wasn't much time before the Borda Witch either escaped or defeated the mermaid, so she had to get as far away from the temple as she could before that happened.

A flurry of bubbles escaped when strong

arms wrapped around her, shooting her toward the surface at a much higher rate of speed than she had previously experienced. She looked around, fearful that the Borda Witch had caught up to her but there was nobody there. Almost before she knew what was happening, she was propelled out of the water, flung more than ten feet vertically into the air before falling again to land with a solid and painful thump in the wooden boat. The familiar geyser of water splashed down around her, telling her all that she needed to know about her rescuer.

"Thanks, Laasya," she said as she tugged off the shell band. She flopped back against one of the seats, exhausted from the swimming she had done and the fear of what had happened. How had the Borda Witch found her? Had she been followed somehow? Worse, had there been a spy within Ceara Temple, someone who had told the witch of her arrival? "Was that how she'd known I was there?"

She had no doubts on why the witch had been sent to Ceara Temple, she had been there for Morgan. The trap had been placed and she had walked, or rather swam, directly into it and yet another of her friends had been caught in the middle of it. How many more times was this going to happen? Why was she always the one running away while the fey she was supposed to protect stayed behind?

As the boat headed for shore, Morgan wiped the moisture from her eyes, trying to convince herself that it was all from the ocean beneath her, and unrolled the scroll once more. It was crumpled, clenched in her fist during her escape from the temple but thankfully undamaged. She looked closely at the drawing of the necklace, searching for anything that would tell her how to get it away from its current owner.

19

GATHERING THE ALLIES

She woke when she bumped against the shore, somewhat surprised that she had slept that long. While the rocking of the waves had lulled her to sleep, she had slept lightly, fully expecting to be attacked on the way.

One thing she had decided almost immediately was that she was done running. She had lost too many people, had seen harm come to too many of her friends, and the damage had simply become too great for her to continue the way she had been going. Figuring out how to stop Eurale was only one part of the bigger problem. The gorgon was just the latest challenge sent out to get in her way. What she needed to focus on was stopping the source of all these challenges, to go directly to the head of the problem.

She needed to stop Ameil.

Ameil Bas-Grann was the single most dangerous threat, not just to herself but also to all of the fey. He had been steadily building his forces and increasing the strength of his attack and she had always been one step behind him, if not more. More than that, Morgan was just plain tired of chasing after him. All of her time was dedicated to survival, to recovering from whatever he and his minions threw at her, so she never had enough time or mental focus to come up with a way to stop him directly. That was something that needed to change, and to change quickly. She needed to become, in the words of her mother, proactive instead of reactive. As far as she could tell, that meant that it was her turn to strike and for Ameil to figure out how to defend against her.

She just needed to figure out how to do that.

She was already deep in thought, brows

thoroughly furled, as she climbed onto Askel's back. The first thing she needed to do was to take stock of what allies she had left. Many of them, she was sure, were already hard at work on trying to figure out a way to restore all of those who had been petrified but she couldn't imagine that all of feykind was on that particular assignment. "We're not going home quite yet," she finally broke the silence.

"High Council?"

"Nope." She shook her head. "I need to contact the Mirror Man."

The gryphon below her twitched at her statement, likely in surprise. It was far more of a reaction than Askel normally had to her words. "Nobody knows where he is," he reminded her gently. "How do you expect to contact him?"

"I need to go to his keep. He's got to have a way to contact him in there." His home in the fey world, even more than the house he had lived at in the human world, was filled with mirrors. While some of those had been transported to his human home, she was certain that there were more powerful ones that had been left behind. Hopefully, one of those would do what she needed.

"Are you certain about this?"

"I am. I don't think I've ever been so certain about anything before now."

"Does this have anything to do with whatever happened at Ceara Temple?"

"Not exactly. The Borda Witch attacked while I was there, I'm sure you've already heard about that, but this is a little different." She set her jaw and took a deep breath, trying to appear braver than she actually felt. Determination was one thing, bravery was another. "We've been playing their game for too long. It's their game, so they've held all the cards. No wonder they've been winning and we've just been running around, trying to pick up any pieces we can find. I think it's time we stopped playing by their rules. It's time to go on the offensive."

"If you are certain of that." Askel accepted her decision and changed direction. Although he had not been allowed to accompany her the first time she had been to the home of the Mirror Man, he had brought her there at a later time when she had tried to return the Cup of

Jamshid. "Do I need to let anyone know of your change in plans?"

"We can start contacting them once we arrive. Right now, I'm still trying to figure out what the plan is going to be."

"You do not know what you plan to do?"

"I'm kinda making it up as we go," she chuckled. "Stormshock kept telling me to follow my instincts and I've been doing a really bad job about that. But I do know that the first thing I need to do is figure out who we have left that can help and figure out how to contact each of them." Not for the first time, she wished Tilson was with her. Not only was he her most constant companion, seconded only by Askel himself, but the haltija had always managed to find a way to contact anyone he needed to. For the longest time, Morgan had wondered how he did it until she had finally spotted him using a tiny gem to speak with the council. It was just too bad that she didn't have a gem like that of her own.

That idea irritated her just as much as anything else lately had. There were so many times where she had needed something, where she had needed assistance with something, but had been unable to contact anyone to ask for help. She had no idea why she hadn't been given any sort of communication device to reach the fey, particularly since Leander, the chosen who had served the same group of fey before her, had been given one. His had been taken away when he was removed as a chosen but while he was a chosen he had gotten one. Not just that, but he had been immediately taught magic as well, something that Morgan herself had been fighting for and had only recently gained permission to learn, for as much good as that had done. With everything that had been going on, her magical training was severely lacking but that was beside the point. Had they taught her as they had taught all of the other chosen, a lot of things would have been much easier. Perhaps, she suspected, they may not be in the bind they currently found themselves in if she had even known the most rudimentary spells.

"Why am I being targeted so directly?" she asked finally. "I mean, I get that Ameil is pretty mad that I've been in the way a bit, but shouldn't he be going after the other chosen, too? It seems like he's putting a lot of effort into stopping me specifically."

"What do you mean?"

"I know Leander was a chosen before me. And I know that Tellius and Lothar were both chosen once upon a time, too. I think Tilson once mentioned that there were lots of other councils out there like the one on Zea Island, but nobody has said anything about all of the other chosen for the other councils. Do you think that any of them would be able to help too, if we contacted them?"

"That will not be possible."

"Why not?"

"Well," the gryphon corrected himself, "I suppose Lothar and Leander could be available and it is likely they would both be willing to assist in whatever manner they are able, particularly after the attack upon Tellius. But I believe those are the extent of the help you can either ask or expect of the chosen, past or present."

"Why only them? They're both former chosen, what about the current ones?"

"Had you not been told?"

"Told what?"

"You are the last. All of the other chosen have been defeated. You are all that remains."

Morgan felt the blood rushing from her body, sinking like a stone thrown into the ocean. Her entire body grew cold, even colder than it had felt at the bottom of the ocean, a coldness that even her ring of protection wouldn't have been able to stop. If it hadn't been for Askel's quick maneuvers, she likely would have fallen completely from his back, the first time she had ever even come close to doing so. "What do you mean they've all been defeated?"

"Your assumption that you were the only one being targeted was incorrect. Ameil targeted you, that is true, but he targeted the rest of the chosen as well. Most of them were defeated months ago. The last was defeated a handful of weeks ago. You are the only one who yet remains."

Morgan thought in silence for a long moment. "Is that why I was brought in as the High Council's chosen?"

"Partly. One of the reasons, you are correct, was that there was no other option. However,

I suspect that you had been groomed for that position for some time now."

"Groomed?" She wasn't sure she liked the way that sounded.

"You were introduced to the Ancients early on," he explained. "Many of them had not met a human in hundreds of years, even longer in some cases. I believe those introductions were not just intended to assist you in your challenges but also to give the Ancients themselves a chance to develop their own opinions of you."

She had heard a few times before that not many chosen had been to meet some of the Ancients but she hadn't recognized the importance of those events. "I hadn't realized," she admitted finally.

"Most of them took a shine to you," Askel continued. "None so much as the Mirror Man, of course, but even Amahté-Baki seemed to be in favor of you. Even many of the Ancients' guardians view you favorably."

That was yet another surprise to Morgan. Sure, she knew that she had a close relationship with the Mirror Man but she hadn't realized that the Egyptian sphynx had been fond

of her as well. At the same time as that knowledge heartened her, she was also hurt yet again
by it. Recently, Amahté-Baki had been attacked
and currently stood as a golden statue in her
lair. She hoped that whenever a restorative was
found for the rest of the fey, it could be used to
restore her as well. "Wait, their guardians?"

"Sure. You remember the ghirtablili, I assume."

She did indeed. "You think he approves of
me too?"

"You did release him from his captivity,"
Askel reminded her. "The very fact that he
allowed you to get as close as you did, weapon
in hand, no less, speaks volumes."

Their conversation took up much of the
travel time from the Atlantic Ocean to the Mirror Man's mountainous keep. They landed in
the massive courtyard, near the spear-blooming
tree but not close enough for Askel's wings to be
damaged by it. Morgan slipped to the ground,
staff and satchel in hand, and headed for the
doorway that led into the Mirror Man's living
space.

Just as it had been previously, the door

was heavy and difficult to push. Either she had grown stronger or the door had been loosened somewhat from the few visits she had made, she wasn't sure which, but it wasn't as difficult to open as she remembered.

The room was darker than she remembered it and somehow felt more oppressive. The shadowed areas seemed to loom threateningly, as though creatures hidden within them were waiting to pounce. Mirrors covered every surface, even more than what was present in his human home. Some of them were missing, brought with him when he left, she supposed, but the biggest ones remained in place. She settled her belongings onto a table, careful to not disturb any of its contents, and turned to survey the room. "I don't even know which one to start with," she said quietly.

"Do you know how to activate it once it is located?"

That was the second problem she would need to face. "No," she admitted. She had never used the mirrors to communicate, so she hadn't learned the trick. Much as she had wanted to ask Nathan about it, it had seemed intrusive and she hadn't asked. Now, she wished she had.

Suddenly, familiar blue eyes met her own, blinking slowly in recognition. They stayed fixed on her for a long moment before turning to view something on the opposite side of the room. Understanding it was a signal from the mirror's owner, she turned to see what he indicated.

A massive mirror, easily the largest of all of them, leaned against a wall, partially covered by a garnet-colored cloth. Certain that this was what he had been wanting her to see, she carefully lifted the cloth away to reveal the mirror beneath.

Nathan stood on the other side, appearing much as he had the last time she had seen him. "Nathan!" she cried, stepping forward.

"It is merely an image of me," he explained, his voice as calm and quiet as always. "Nevertheless, I am pleased indeed to see you. Particularly since you appear to remain unharmed." His smile faltered as he added, "I worried for you."

"I've been worried about you too," she said. "Where are you? Askel and I can come get you."

He shook his head. "It is far too dangerous for you to come here. I am safe, at least for the time being, but you would not be. Ameil Bas-Grann has far too many of his followers placed around me. You would certainly not be success-ful in coming here and leaving again safely." He smiled again. "Do not worry for me. They be-lieve me to be trapped but that is not the case."

As badly as she wanted to crawl through the mirror and drag him back home, she knew that he was probably right. If Ameil knew how close he and Morgan were, he was probably expect-ing her to come to his rescue. "So what do we do?"

"You will need assistance," he suggested. "I believe you and Askel already began discussions on this matter."

"How could you possibly know that?"

"The clouds," his eyes twinkled as he re-sponded. "The water droplets contained within them are small but reflective."

"The clouds." Her voice was flat as she re-peated his words. "Of course." This wasn't the first time she had seen him use the air itself as a reflective surface, although the first time she had seen it, she hadn't realized that the boy she had met was actually the Mirror Man.

"You may use my mirrors to communicate with your companions," he offered. "The one to your left will work just as the one that currently resides in Ceara Temple."

Morgan looked at the mirror, recognizing it as a very close copy of the one she had already seen. "At least tell me where you are," she relented. "Once I have backup, we'll come for you."

He explained where he was being held. It wasn't an area that she recognized but when she glanced to see if Askel knew of the place, the gryphon nodded. "Okay. But you be careful while you're there and let me know if anything changes, anything at all."

He agreed and faded from view so she turned to the smaller mirror. She recited the incantation he had shown her, completing it with Leander's name. "Hopefully he's near a mirror," she said as the glass turned cloudy. Within seconds, an image of Leander formed and she smiled at him in greeting. "How are things going out there?"

"About the same," he smiled in return. "I see you found the Mirror Man."

"Not exactly. But I'm in his house and he's letting me play with his toys." She began explaining about her plan to launch a rescue mission to retrieve him.

Before she was done speaking, he interrupted her. "When do we leave?"

"You're my first call, so I still need to see who else I can get ahold of. Once I figure out what I have to work with, we can start on the next phase of the plan."

After speaking with him for a few minutes longer, mostly just to get caught up on how Lothar was doing and to wave at him when he appeared behind Leander, she ended the spell and immediately cast again. She contacted Stormshock and Magicgleam but neither of the dragons would be able to help. "We are needed here," Stormshock explained. "Much as we would love to go, we cannot." Just as she had suspected, the veil had been thinning over recent weeks and all of the dragons who remained had combined forces across the world to maintain it as best they could.

Disappointed but unfazed, she tried a few more people she knew and her forces steadily grew larger. Not only was she reaching out to those she knew through Nathan's mirrors, but Askel was receiving information from others as they volunteered to join her quest. A beast-rider who Morgan hadn't ever met before agreed to join, along with his polar bear mount. A handful of peri volunteered, much to Morgan's surprise. Remembering what she had been told by the peri who had so recently come to her house, she hoped their magic was as powerful as they said it would be. If things worked out the way she expected, they would need it. Particularly now that she knew the dragons would be sitting this one out.

"On the one hand, it's surprising to me," she explained to Askel while she took a break between conversations. "So many are eager to come out and fight with us. Some of them, it almost seems as though they've been waiting for someone to call them to action, like they've just been waiting for me to be ready."

"They lack a leader," the gryphon explained. "Many of those who we regularly follow have been killed, have been turned to stone, or are otherwise unavailable for one reason or another. Many have been wanting to do something about all this but have been unable to do so on their own."

Morgan looked around the Mirror Man's small living space. "So many things could have stopped all of this before it got this far. I really wish I could have done better from the beginning."

"You have done well and you should be proud of what you have accomplished. Everyone has setbacks on occasion so there is no reason for you to feel such guilt over things such as this." Askel looked thoughtful for a moment before adding, "I believe your people have a phrase for feelings such as what you are experiencing."

"What's that?"

"You are only human."

She chuckled and nodded. "I'd expected you to say something wise, as you always do. I should have suspected you'd have something like that. But to be honest, I would have more expected that from Liore."

"She has much wisdom to offer as well. But, I am certain you are already aware of that."

When she reached out to the Irusan, he was already waiting for her call. "The oracle told us what you are doing," he explained. "I have extended the invitation to those available from my tribe. Five of my cats are ready and willing to aid you."

When she finished reaching out to everyone she could think of, asking them all to meet on Zea Island, she sat back thoughtfully for a moment. While there were a couple others who she could contact, such as Nitsa and Laasya, she decided against it. Their destination was above ground, so the water-based fey would be of little assistance.

Once she was done with her calls, Morgan looked over at the large mirror once more, wondering whether Nathan would make another appearance. After watching for almost a full minute, she decided that he wasn't going to show, so she turned back to Askel. "Time to go."

They arrived on Zea Island just after sunrise

and she was amazed to see just how many had arrived. Not only those she had been expecting, but there were a few others with whom she had been unable to make contact. A group of gnomes had joined the party, as had a pair of giants, one of whom she recognized. Kun had been guarding Cinderflare's lair the night Morgan became a chosen. She smiled at him sheepishly in recognition, slightly ashamed that she hadn't given him much thought since those first handful of nights. Lothar had invited the black pegasus stallion that she had met previously, who was visibly eager to join the fight. A few satyrs waited in the clearing as well, along with countless others that she couldn't identify.

"Here's the plan," she explained as they landed. "The Mirror Man has been captured by Ameil Bas-Grann. He's being held in one of Ameil's strongholds under heavy guard. We have to expect that they're expecting us to come and there are a lot of them to defend the place when we get there." She looked out at the gathered crowd and swallowed. She had never spoken in front of this many people before and it was a little daunting. Straightening her back, she dug deep and continued. "He is about a three-hour flight away from here but I know not all of you can fly, so Askel and I decided on a meeting spot that should be far enough away from the stronghold for all of us to gather without them knowing. We can launch our attack from there. Any questions?"

"Yeah," an apotharni she didn't recognize spoke up. "When do we leave?"

20

ASSAULT ON AMEIL

The staging area they had selected was in a valley downstream from Ameil's base. Morgan and Askel were the first to arrive, quickly joined by an increasing number of fey. Airborne fey flew in, some carrying passengers who could not travel as quickly. Underground fey tunneled. Some were transported from one area to the next by means that Morgan couldn't identify, likely spells and magical items of some variety. Some of the arrivals brought even more allies with them, as made apparent by the enormous swarm of peri who darkened the sky upon arrival. Vouivre and a half dozen identical wyverns carried multiple fey each on their backs. Tekli and his fellow cats delivered a passenger each. Glau brought another pair of gryphons, neither of whom had Morgan previously met. Elvor, gnomes, peri, satyrs, beastriders and more continued to flock into the area. Soon, the silent valley was filled with excited chattering and nervous tittering.

"Are you certain of this?" Corran came to see Morgan after his arrival. "We know nothing of what is beyond the outer wall."

While still in the Mirror Man's keep, Morgan had spent a bit of time debating on whether to include Corran on her initial invitations. She still wasn't sure she trusted the elvor but he hadn't done anything overt enough for her to truly question him and leaving him off of the invitation list would have been suspicious on her part. The only real evidence she had of his deception had come from her amulet, which told her he had lied to her. That information, particularly when coupled with Stormshock's suspicions that there was a traitor within the council, had caused her biggest issue with Corran. Despite her own reservations about him, she had ultimately decided to include him. Better to keep him close where she could keep an eye on him, she supposed. Her only real concern had been whether he would tell Ameil of her plans and the assault on his stronghold. In the end, however, she had decided the risk was worthwhile. If Corran wasn't a traitor, his magic and other abilities could prove useful and she didn't want to cause an unnecessary rift between them.

"True," she admitted, "but the Mirror Man has given me a lot of information on what to expect when we get inside."

The elvor's face reflected his surprise at her words. "You have been in contact with him?"

She nodded. "I went to his place and spoke to him through one of his mirrors. That's how we knew where this place was and that he's inside."

"So this is less of an assault on Bas-Grann," he mused, "and more of a rescue mission."

"It's a little bit of both. We're pretty sure Ameil is inside so we may be able to kill two birds with one stone here."

Corran's expression of surprise turned to

confusion. "Why are we killing birds?" He turned to scan the trees. "Are they in league with our adversary?"

Morgan had to chuckle. She often forgot that Corran didn't have as much direct experience with the human world as most of the fey she dealt with regularly. "It's just an expression," she said. "The birds are fine."

"Do we know what manner of beasts lie inside?"

"He wasn't as sure on that, so he only told me about the ones he had spotted. He's seen a bunch of minotaurs, so we know those are going to be a problem again. There are also some strange spider creatures, which he described as half-man, half-spider, kinda like the spider version of a centaur."

"I have heard of those," Corran nodded. "As I understand, they are quite poisonous."

"Oh goody, just what we were hoping for." She hoped that her voice conveyed the irony she intended. "He described some sort of a flaming demon-looking thing and a bunch of lizards. He was pretty clear those weren't dragons, or even wyverns, just lizards."

"That is of little help, there are many varieties of lizards known to humans and fey."

Morgan fell quiet as she finished the list, knowing there was another type of fey Nathan had told her about but unsure of how the elvor would respond when she told him. Finally, she said, "He says there are more elvor inside, too."

"Elvor? You are certain of this?"

"Mhmm. He said there were at least three that he has seen so far. Corran, I..."

"Worry not," he interrupted her. His voice was much harder than she had heard it in a long time. "If any of my brethren have turned traitor, they are no longer worthy of your concern. Need be, I will be the first to strike them down."

After she finished talking with Corran, Morgan went from group to group of the gathered fey, checking in with everyone to see if they were all ready and to find out whether any were still waiting on more reinforcements. Many were nervous, as she herself was, so she spent time talking with them in the hopes of reassuring them all as best she could.

It was going to be dangerous, of that she

had no doubts whatsoever. She remembered Nathan's warning, informing her that the base was heavily guarded and her chances of survival were low. As she looked around those who had gathered at her call, she wondered how many of them would make it out alive. She reflected back on some of the history classes she had attended, where they learned about and discussed stories of armies marching against reinforced strong-holds. Some of the armies had been success-ful, achieving victories against their opponents. Other stories told of defeat, of the defending forces managing to beat the odds and hold out against invasion. From what she could tell, the history books really liked an underdog story, so she was curious to find out which she would end up being. Was her group the underdog? If they were, could they be strong enough to break through, to rescue Nathan, and to defeat Ameil?

"You appear deep in thought," Leander came to check on her. "I understand you're concerned about this plan of yours."

"What if we lose?" she asked, her voice

barely above a whisper. "What if none of us make it out?"

"Those are two different things," he reminded her. "If we lose, we retreat and come up with a new plan."

She looked again at the ragtag group of fey. "Are these really all we have left to stand against him?"

He shook his head. "Absolutely not. These are only the ones who were able to come on short notice. Plenty of others stand behind you, they just weren't able to make it out here today."

What he said made sense and reassured her a little. She couldn't have expected every fey across the planet to have come to join her. They all had their own work to do, their own assignments. "I think everyone's here," she said finally. "At least, everyone who's coming. I haven't seen any more show up in about a half hour or so."

Leander nodded. "You ready for this?"

She smiled with only half of her mouth. "Is there really any way to be ready for this?" She headed for the edge of the clearing closest to the base. "*Vluchten.*" The word activated the flying necklace Leander had given to her, the one that was identical to the one he still wore. She rose into the air until she was high enough to see and be seen by everyone in the area.

In the movies she often watched back home, this was the scene where the leader of the force gave a motivating speech to get everyone fired up for the battle to come. But this wasn't a movie and she was hardly a leader, so she just raised her arms to get everyone's attention. Below her, everyone turned to face her, a field of expectant eyes. "Ameil Bas-Grann's stronghold lies just over that ridge," she pointed. "He and his people have been attacking us for months, years, if not longer. One of our own is being held inside, kept away from all of us. Today, we have the opportunity to put a stop to all of this, to keep more of our people from being harmed by him and his forces. We cannot undo what has already been done but, right now, we can stop it from continuing. You guys ready to go?"

A clamor rose from the crowd, louder and more excited than she had expected. A wild smile played across her face as she realized that she had done it. It may have not been the most motivating of speeches, but she'd done it. "Well then," she called out, "let's go!"

The howling, screaming force swarmed over the ridge and toward the keep. As she approached, Morgan got a good look at the stronghold for the first time.

Mist swirled around the building, whether natural or otherwise, she couldn't tell. The main structure was two stories tall and formed of black bricks, with what appeared to be the remnants of a bell tower on top toward the back. Part of the front of the building had crumbled, leaving massive holes in the exterior. An eerie red glow emanated from the bottom floor of the structure, flickering slightly in the haze. Some of the fey ran toward the arched opening, others flew into the gaps in the stonework.

Morgan flew in through the front archway, not wanting to get in the way of the rampaging wyverns, who appeared to be starting from the top, ripping pieces of the roof away in their haste to gain entry.

The first thing she saw when she got into the building were a handful of minotaurs, each of which looked exactly like the one she had encountered in the underground caverns. They held weapons, massive clubs that looked like nothing less than lengths of uprooted trees, which they swung with massive power at the invading force. As she watched, one of them leaned forward and used his enormous horns to scoop up an elvor and fling him aside like nothing more than a rag doll. At first, Morgan had thought the flung elvor was Corran, but she soon spotted him some distance away from the fray, flinging spell after spell at the furious beasts.

Deeper into the complex, she found more of the fey tangled with more of Ameil's forces. The man-spider hybrids had slung webbing across a massive area, webbing that had already trapped over a dozen peri. Fearful and remembering how it had felt when she herself had been trapped in webbing similar to that, Morgan darted into the action, plucking peri after peri away from the sticky webbing. Just as she released the fifth one, a jet of olive-green spray shot past her, barely missing her skin. She let go of the freed peri and turned to face the creature that had caused the spray.

One of the spider creatures had snuck up behind her while she was busy. It stepped carefully across the floor, its eight legs making no sound as it moved. Tiny black hairs grew off of its legs, sending a shudder of disgust down Morgan's spine. Above all else, no matter how disgusting or icky some of the things she had encountered so far had been, the ones she liked the least were spiders. Always had been, always would be. The creature advancing on her was no different, despite the human-looking portion of its body.

It was smaller than she had expected, shorter than even she was. The last spider she had encountered, the Djieien, had been absolutely enormous, far dwarfing her in size. This one appeared to be only over half her height, although she didn't want to consider how far out its legs could stretch. As she watched, it pulled its head back as though preparing to spit the vile fluid at her again.

"Nope," she muttered. "We're not playing this game today." She choked up on her staff, activated one of the functions, and swung. She had no clue what the green goo it spat towards her would do but she wasn't interested in the slightest in finding out.

The end furthest away from her hands unfurled into three parts, which she normally used as it was intended, to grab at things that were just outside of her reach. Now, she used the end of her staff as a claw, swiping at the beast's face and leaving deep gouges in its upper chest and face. It skittered back, increasing the distance between itself and her offense, an offense it obviously hadn't been expecting.

"You can just back off, you ugly, disgusting thing." Morgan swung at it again, and then a third time, keeping a wary eye out for more of the monstrous creatures. This one had been silent, sneaking up on her as it approached, and she didn't want others to take this opportunity to do the same. Twice she changed direction of her attack, ensuring that none of the spider beasts came within her range.

Undeterred, one of them spat at her, launching a stream of the foul liquid in her direction. She only barely dodged the attack, stepping out of the way and watching as the spittle crossed through the area she had occupied only a second previously.

"*Vlam!*" A voice called out from the other end of the room. The spider creatures erupted into fire, engulfed in the massive fireball that filled the room.

Morgan shrieked at the assault, dropping to the ground in order to stay below the fire level and wondering what fresh nightmare had joined the fray. Footsteps calmly approached and she looked up apprehensively until she recognized the torn jeans and dirty red sweatshirt belonging to Leander.

"Looked like you could use a hand in here," he said. Soot covered his clothes, indicating that this had not been the first fireball he had unleashed. "You okay?"

"I think so." She pushed herself to her feet, checking for damage. "Yeah, I'm fine." She looked over at where the spiders had fallen, curled up in balls of death. "Thanks for that."

"Figured fire worked well on the last spider that attacked you," he shrugged. "We should get moving, though There's a lot of area to cover still."

She agreed and they headed deeper into the building.

The room grew both warmer and brighter as the red glow from ahead intensified. As Morgan pushed up the sleeves of her sweatshirt to relieve some of the warmth, not quite willing to completely forego the small amount of protection it offered, a blazing, blackened creature appeared.

Its body, at least as far as Morgan could tell, was a mass of burned, charred flesh roughly shaped like a human. She couldn't even tell whether it was male or female, not that it mattered. Horns grew from its head, glistening black and curved slightly backwards. Yellow amber eyes stared malevolently as it approached, revealing no semblance of either fear or caution. Flames licked across its body, zigzagging from head to toe and back again as it stepped, slowly and calmly, into the room.

"That must be the demon thing the Mirror Man mentioned," Leander said.

"Looks like it. That's what I'd call it, at least." One thing she was certain about, she knew that Leander's fireball would have little, if any, effect on this creature. "What's the opposite of fireball?"

Leander furled his brows in thought. "Water spout, I'd guess. Either that or ice storm."

"I don't suppose you know either of those, do you?" When he shook his head in response, she sighed. She had the ring that protected her against cold but she doubted it would be useful against fire. The armband of water breathing was even less helpful, as it didn't generate water, it just allowed her to breathe it. At one point, Arien had given her a jar of salve to keep her safe against the heat of an active volcano, but that jar had broken long ago and she hadn't ever asked for a replacement, an oversight she could kick herself for now. As the fiery demon approached, sending a wall of flame before it, she wracked her brain to think of what to do.

"Should we try to find another way around?" Worry tinged Leander's voice, confirming that he was out of ideas as well.

"Yeah."

As they turned to find a different path, the demon shrieked. Its scream was loud enough to force Morgan to cover her ears in an attempt to muffle the sound. Next to her, Leander reacted in much the same way, flinching and backing away.

As the creature screamed, Morgan's insides twisted up in agony, searing heat blasting through her entire body as though ignited in her very core and seeking a way out. She dropped to a knee in pain, her own screams joining the demonic howls. Her skin felt as though it was about to tear completely away from her and every muscle throughout her body began to cramp, violently and painfully. Waves of dizziness and nausea cascaded over her, pain adding to pain adding to pain with every second that ticked by.

"Morgan," a voice broke through the blinding, mind-numbing pain. She couldn't identify it but it echoed through her brain as though it had originated there. Had her mind been any clearer, she would have wondered if it was nothing more than her own imagination.

"Morgan!" The voice grew louder, demanding her attention. She felt herself moving, being dragged across the floor by unseen hands. Slowly, the pain faded and her mind cleared.

When she opened her eyes again, she found herself in a different room, Leander leaning over her and shaking her a bit more roughly than her cramping muscles appreciated. "Morgan!"

"I'm okay," she whimpered, memories of the pain not quite faded. She sucked in a deep, shuddering breath and wrapped her arms around herself protectively. "What was that?"

"It was just like Avekaine's wail," Leander explained. "Remember how you needed protection to get close enough to her?"

"This was nothing like her." The cyhyraeth had caused pain, certainly, but the pain she had caused was emotional. Her cries had brought forth a deep, aching despair. The demon's cry had been nothing less than the torture of hell itself.

"Same basic principle. Different creatures have different effects."

Even though she had agreed to find a different way around the demonic creature, Morgan already knew that they would have to figure out a way to overcome it. Anything that powerful, she was certain, guarded Ameil himself. "So how do we get past that?"

"Earplugs could work," Leander suggested. "They work against sirens, so they should work against that. I'm pretty sure that was a sonic attack."

"Sirens?"

"Yeah. I'll explain about those later. Do you have anything that can plug your ears?"

Morgan dug in her satchel for a moment before coming back up with nothing. "About the only thing I could use is the blanket but I don't have anything to cut it with."

"I can help with that." Leander pulled a small folding knife from his pocket and offered it to her. "You really should start carrying one of these, they're super handy."

"I'll keep that in mind." As she cut a pair of small squares from the wool cloth, something else caught her attention. "Think this is a magical creature?"

"What else could it be?"

Morgan nodded and pulled a thin stick out of her satchel.

"Whoa," Leander breathed. "You still have that?"

"Yup. And I bet you it will hurt it."

She stuffed the squares of cloth into her ears and handed the knife back to Leander. The makeshift earplugs blocked out most of the sound, so she pushed herself back to her feet, warily looking around to ensure that nothing was sneaking up on them. The last thing she needed to contend with at that moment was a sneaky spider. With a nod to Leander, she headed toward the demon.

It had crossed almost halfway through the room in the time they were gone. Without waiting for a repeat performance, Morgan raised the wand and pointed it at the demon. "*Heilig Verlich.*" A beam of pure white light shot out of the stick as she finished speaking, cutting through the flames and hitting the demon directly in the chest.

Normally, she had learned, the wand only did a moderate amount of holy damage. This did nothing against natural creatures but it was more than enough to drive away most of the magical creatures that could be found. In this case, however, Morgan had a secret weapon up her sleeve, in the most literal sense possible. A series of tiny, thin strands of silver metal, set with an assortment of gemstones, was stuck on her upper arm just above the elbow, ensured to remain in place by magic Morgan could not break. That piece of unusual jewelry was known as an amplifier and it increased the output of magic by a substantial amount. Because of that, the beam of light did more than the usual amount of damage. Much more.

When it impacted, it flung the demon backwards, through the doorway by which it had entered the room. Morgan advanced quickly, blasting at the creature again as she moved. Screaming in anger, frustration, and pain, Morgan fired again and again until, after the fourth beam, the demon stopped moving and the flames began to extinguish.

A hand on her arm brought her back to her senses and she lowered her arm. Breathing heavily, she stepped around the fallen demon.

She didn't look at it as she passed. This wasn't the first time she had been forced to kill one of the fey and it was unlikely to be the last. Much as she didn't like it, she understood that at times it was necessary. With everything else that had been going on, she had more important things to focus on than her own morality. With the demon down, Ameil was her next target. She just needed to find him and put a stop to this madness.

She pulled the cloth from her ears and turned to Leander. "Let's go."

His eyes filled with concern, he nodded.

Despite her confidence that Ameil Bas-Grann waited in the next room, or at least the next series of rooms, he was nowhere to be found. As they ascended to the second floor, she encountered a group of fey coming down them, Nathan in tow. She rushed forward to hug him, thankful that he appeared unharmed.

"What of Bas-Grann?" One of the fey with him inquired. "Has he been stopped?"

Morgan shook her head. "Not that I've heard yet. We haven't seen any sign of him down here. If you guys came from upstairs, I assume that means he's not up there either."

They spent the next half hour ensuring that none of the stronghold's guardians remained. Scorched walls and floors showed as clear evidence that Leander hadn't been the only one using fire spells but melting stalactites showed that other types of magic were used as well. One of the walls appeared to have been temporary transformed into a stone golem, now motionless. Green fluid, remnants of spider bile, pooled on the floor and Morgan was careful to avoid it. She didn't know if the vile liquid remained poisonous after the spiders were dead but she wasn't interested in finding out.

"You should be pleased," Corran, soot smeared across his face and into his hair, came to greet her as they left the building. "You have accomplished much this night."

"Not everything," Morgan answered. "Ameil wasn't here. And neither was Eurale." While she had all of the information she could hope for in order to defeat the gorgon, Morgan still wasn't sure on her ability to actually win in a fight against her. Disappointed that the petrification attacks could continue, she had a difficult time accepting the battle as having been successful.

"True. But we will keep our eyes and ears open for any signs of him. However," he looked around at the group of survivors, "you accomplished much, even though not all you had hoped for. Perhaps it is time we leave this place.

Until Bas-Grann's true location is identified, there is little else here for us to do and some of the wounded need tending to."

Morgan agreed. To her surprise and relief, almost all of the fey who had joined her on the assault made it back out safely... but not all of them. A gryphon, two satyrs, and many peri had been lost in the battle. When she had first heard of the lost gryphon, her first thoughts had been for Askel and Glau, but she was relieved to see them both among the survivors. As Corran climbed onto Glau's back, she went over to bury her face in Askel's feathers. Even though Ameil's forces had been diminished in her assault, it had cost lives.

Just as she had feared it would.

~ 21 ~

RESTORATIVE

When she arrived back at her house, Morgan knew immediately that something was not quite right. The house was too quiet, the windows too dark. As she carefully stepped through the familiar rooms, she spotted her parents, sitting on the couch watching television as they were prone to do in the evenings. Letting out a sigh of relief, she headed past them toward her room before stopping.

Something was wrong.

She turned back to face her parents, slowly advancing on them. As she got closer, she discovered that neither of them was moving at all. She reached out a hand to touch them, already knowing what she would find. Her fingertips confirmed her worst suspicions. Where soft clothing and smooth skin should have been, they touched nothing more than unyielding stone.

"Think of it as a gift," a voice spoke behind her. "Now you no longer need to sneak through your own home."

Morgan whirled around in shock, almost falling directly into the gorgon's trap. The second she spotted the scaly form, she squeezed her eyes closed, praying she had been fast enough. "They have nothing to do with any of this," she said, her voice far calmer than she truly was.

"That may be true," Eurale agreed, "but you are a chosen. That means that one of them was a chosen as well."

Her words were true. David Lafayette, mild-mannered bank employee, had once been a chosen, years before Morgan had been selected to became one. "Not anymore." She cast quick glances around, trying to figure out how to defeat the gorgon. She caught her reflection in the glass of one of the many framed photographs that her mother had all over the living room and confirmed that Eurale still wore the Necklace of Harmonia. The snake-headed clasp was in front of her, below the gorgon's chin, so Morgan knew she had a chance. She just needed to figure out how to get it away from her.

"There is, of course, another option."

"What's that?" If Morgan could keep her talking, it should give her enough time to come up with some sort of a plan.

"Your decision is simple. You can either continue to fight against us, or you can stop fighting. The Meister has already decided that any who wish to join him will be welcomed."

"Oh yeah? And how many have accepted that offer?"

Eurale laughed. "Quite a few, actually. Far more than I had expected. But that is the nature of the fey. So fickle."

"What's in it for me?"

As they spoke, Morgan slowly crept closer to the gorgon, keeping up the pretense of not knowing where the snake-woman was. She kept a firm hold on her staff, maneuvering her fingers to reach the activation sigils. This, she was certain, was likely to be her only shot. The multitude of photographs gave her ample reflective surfaces to navigate and her living room wasn't so large as to give Eurale much room to maneuver, given the length of her tail. One thing that her time with the fey had taught her, particularly when working with Vouivre, was that bigger didn't automatically mean better. In most cases, being too large was more of a hindrance than a benefit. She just hoped that the same logic held true for the snake woman.

"You get to live. Not just live but to thrive, as by accepting his offer you will receive more power than you could have ever possibly gotten as just a simple chosen."

"It's tempting." Her fingers found the sigil and pressed it. She could feel the slight vibration in the staff as it unfurled. Never before had she considered using the staff this way, at least not intentionally, but this was hardly the first time she had used it for something the druids who built it and gave it to her had ever intended. She had lost count of how many times she had used her staff as a makeshift baseball bat and she had once used it in order to vault herself from one place to another. So far, it had held up to all manner of abuses, so she hoped it would withstand one more. "What kind of power?"

"Why, magical power, of course. We already have control of some of the most powerful artifacts known to feykind, most of them in fact. And the rest will fall under our control soon enough. You will have your choice of which artifacts you desire for yourself."

Morgan considered her offer. She remembered the feel of Tilson, his small stone form feeling so helpless and fragile in her arms. She remembered waking up to discover all of her friends turned to stone, the horror she had felt when she realized she was the only survivor. The recognition that one of her friends had sacrificed himself so that she could live. So that she could save them. So that she could stop this horrible creature who continued to laugh at them, to insult them, to demean them in any way that she could. Eurale, she decided, was a far worse bully than any she had ever even heard of, in her old school or in the new one.

Although it was a close race, she thought the gorgon might even be worse than Ameil.

"Okay," Morgan agreed. "I'm tired of fighting you. I'm tired of watching everyone get turned to stone all the time. I don't want to be turned into stone myself, and I certainly don't want to be killed." She lifted her eyes, not quite high enough to meet the eyes of the gorgon before her but high enough to see the necklace. Just above the chain, the gorgon's mouth twisted upwards in a satisfied smile, obviously pleased at Morgan's words. "So I'm done with all of this." She swung, as hard and as fast as she possibly could, aiming for the golden necklace.

Obviously not expecting this kind of response from her prey, Eurale was slow to react. Even when she did move, she dodged what she believed was an attack on her person. As she backed away, Morgan withdrew the glittering necklace from the end of her staff.

"You little brat!" Eurale shrieked in rage and lunged at her. "Not only will you become stone as your friends, you will be shattered into fragments as soon as it is done. Nothing in this world will be able to save you." Her high, taunting voice lowered as she spoke until the last words came out as nothing more than a sour hiss.

"I don't think so." The necklace snapped around Morgan's neck and she raised her eyes to meet those of her tormentor. Fire burned inside her, pits of rage that had been simmering for months and finally began to erupt. "We're done here." Once again, she swung the staff at the gorgon, lodging one of the hooks into her neck where the protective necklace had been displayed only moments before.

Eurale's eyes widened and she reached up to grasp the staff with both hands but Morgan refused to budge. She leaned against the staff, pushing the gorgon backward toward the kitchen. Her tail flailing about angrily, Eurale couldn't get a good hold on the slippery tile floor.

"I read about this in a book once, years, ago," Morgan explained. "Your sister, I think it was. Medusa. How she was killed." She pushed harder, pressing the gorgon against a wall. Reaching down with her other hand, she opened a drawer, the drawer where she knew her mother kept her set of cooking knives. Without taking her eyes off her captive, Morgan pulled out the first one she laid her hands on.

"The book said that the only way to kill her was to take off her head. I wonder... will that work for you, too?"

"Morgan, stop." A voice called from the other end of the room. Corran, with a woven-reed shade protecting his face from the gorgon's gaze, stepped up next to her. "She need not be killed. We can return her to prison."

"Will you really?" Doubt dripped from Morgan's voice.

"Of course we will." Without seeing his face, the surprise was evident in his words. "What brings about this question?"

"You lied to me before," she explained simply. "So why not lie to me again?"

"When have I lied to you?"

"Stop moving." Morgan turned her attention back to the gorgon. "I still want you dead, so I suggest you stop squirming around so much." She looked back to the elvor. "You said you gave the hammer back to Volcan."

Corran sighed. "I did say that. You are correct."

"That was a lie."

"It was."

"Why would you lie about that?" She turned to face him more fully, maintaining her grip on the staff, just in case Eurale thought there was an opening to escape. "He sent the Djieien after me because of that. You almost got me killed. You almost got Askel and Tilson killed, too. Why didn't you just give it back to him?"

"I tried." Corran sighed. "I was..." he paused before continuing, "unable."

"So why not just tell me the truth?"

"Can we discuss this when we are not holding Eurale at the point of your blade?"

Morgan looked at him for a long moment. Her amulet hadn't indicated any deception from him yet, so she relented. "You swear she will be taken directly to the prison? The one in Hoarfrost Castle?"

"I so swear."

She paused for a heartbeat, followed by another one as she made her decision. "Fine. Go ahead and take her."

At her concession, Corran stepped forward and placed a carved wooden box over Eurale's head. "This is to keep her from being able to attack during transport," he explained. Once the box was secure, he motioned for a group of elvor, many of whom had just come from the assault on Ameil's base. They came in with long poles, similar to the one Morgan held, with heavy iron pieces at the ends. They shackled Eurale's arms and attached the iron circles around her neck so that multiple elvor could lead her away, each of them at a safe distance. Once they and the gorgon were gone, Corran turned back to Morgan and lifted his face covering. "It appears we have much to discuss."

Morgan nodded sullenly. "I don't trust you right now," she said. "Haven't for a long time."

"I had noticed but I knew not why. Now, I would appreciate you telling me what has happened between us."

She shook her head. "First, you tell me why you lied to me and what happened to the hammer. Then I'll tell you what happened."

"Shall we sit, in that case?" He motioned toward the dining room table. "It appears this will be a lengthy conversation."

"First of all," he began once they were both seated at the table, "you should be aware that there has been suspicion throughout my council that one of us was working with Bas-Grann. Unfortunately, I knew not whom and could not point a finger of suspicion at anyone, particularly at someone I considered to be a friend, without some sort of proof."

What he said sounded very similar to the conversation she had held with Stormshock on the same topic but she wasn't willing to simply accept his words at face value. "Why did you think someone from the island was working with him?"

"Simply put, he knew too much and became too powerful in too short of a time. While it has happened in the past that a human has discovered us accidentally and even grew to such power, these instances always occurred over the course of a lifetime, never only over the course of a few short years. It was because of this haste we knew that someone had to have been helping him. It was not until much later, when he began to make himself known here, that we realized that the person helping him had to have been someone within our council. Perhaps not at first but at some point. Bas-Grann knew of our plans and was prepared for every move we made against him."

"Why didn't you tell me any of this? Don't you realize how much danger I was in because I didn't know any of this?"

"I am well aware of the danger I sent you into. Both you and Tilson. But you must realize that you were the only means by which we even stood a chance against him. Nobody would ever suspect that a newly-selected chosen would ever be sent to such places, so they were unprepared for your arrival.

"Moreover, because you had received so little training, your actions were not based on what we had taught you. They were driven solely by your own instincts, which proved to be the most difficult part about you to stop."

"Is that why you didn't want me to learn magic? Because it would change how I reacted to things?" All this time she had been diligently working with all of them, all of the times she had asked about learning one form of magic or another, only to be denied, and this was his reason? It sounded unbelievable but her amulet continued to remain silent, not indicating any deception. She lifted a hand to feel it under her shirt, just to ensure it hadn't disappeared without her realization at some point.

"Precisely. Many of us agreed that you should be given as many magical items as you could possibly need, from the ring of cold resistance to the armband you received from Ceara Temple, to assist you in your dealings. By having choices that could be made, you were free to do as you saw fit in each of these situations. And, I must admit, you surprised even us in some of your actions."

Morgan considered his words, still not certain of how much faith to put in them. "So you've kinda been lying to me the whole time. Maybe not directly, but definitely not telling me everything I needed to know."

"The hammer was just another instance of such. My intent all along was to return the hammer to Volcan but it was stolen before that could be done."

"Stolen? By who?"

"We still do not know. When I told you I returned the hammer, that had indeed been my intent. And, once the location of hammer is uncovered, I still intend to return it."

Morgan sighed. Everything he had said to her made a lot of sense but she still felt as though there was something missing from his explanation. Her amulet had remained quiet throughout his entire story, so she left it alone. She could figure out what to do with all she had learned later, once she'd gotten more time to process it. "Stormshock told me that he thought there was a traitor in the council," she explained. "That was the same time I discovered he was still alive and the reason he gave for why he went into hiding."

Corran smiled wanly. "So you truly did know of his survival for far longer than the rest of us."

Morgan nodded. "He asked me to not tell anyone, so I didn't. But it was just after that, when I finished using the Cup of Jamshid and you wanted me to hand it over to you. My amulet told me you lied, so I thought it might be you." She continued to explain that there were a few other small, not very strong indicators she had seen outside of those, but they had been the biggest reasons for her to be suspicious.

"The last part was when everyone got turned to stone. You weren't there when it happened but you showed up just afterward. It seemed too coincidental."

He nodded. "I can see how that raised your suspicions. But I give you my word I had nothing to do with what happened that day. I was as shocked as you were when I saw what had transpired."

"So where do we go from here?"

"Well, for starters, I will return to the council. Cristin has made great strides toward a means by which we can restore those who have been petrified while we have been elsewhere, so I want to check on his progress." He looked toward the living room, where her parents sat motionless. "Do you wish to remain here, or would you prefer to return with me?"

She thought about it for a long moment. "I don't think I want to stay here," she said finally. "I know Eurale's not coming back, at least I hope she's not, but it's really weird to have them sitting there like that."

"I understand. Askel waits outside, so let us be off."

Morgan spent almost two weeks with the fey, assisting Cristin as best she could but mostly just staying out of the way. One of the first things she discovered upon her return was that Nathan had been returned to his keep in the mountains. It was decided that the human world offered no additional safety than his own home did. Saddened that she wouldn't be able to spend much time with him, at least not for a while yet, she tried to push the thoughts of him from her mind, with little success. She and Corran didn't have another lengthy conversation such as the one they had held in her house, but she was okay with that. She wasn't sure she was ready for another one yet anyway.

It was odd, seeing Stormshock's grotto overrun with fey. Cristin's work area was off to one edge of the clearing and other spaces had been set up for more of the fey to work. The dragon tried to engage her in conversation a few times but she just wasn't feeling up to it.

Finally, a celebratory shout came up from Cristin's area and everyone's attention turned in that direction. "I've got it!" the apotharni shouted. "It works!" A tiny peri, one who had been stone only moments before, fluttered gaily in the air around his head.

Hollers of glee arose from everyone, Morgan included. Finally, it seemed, this part of the nightmare would soon be over. While she understood that Ameil was still out there, still plotting to take control of pretty much everything, hopefully they would have a little bit of time to breathe and recover before his next attack.

"We shall restore the petrified fey," Corran explained later that evening as he brought her a box filled with vials. "I believe it is only proper for you to take care of restoring those in the human world."

She nodded and accepted the box. When Askel headed in her direction, she waved him off. "They probably need you to help distribute the cure among the fey," she said. "I can get back home on my own." She picked up her staff and satchel of belongings, which she had kept packed for just such an announcement, and lifted into the air. "Let me know when you need me again."

Her first stop was her own house, where she

concealed herself beneath her cloak before using a dose on her parents. This was her first time seeing the effects in person and she watched in amazement as the stone began to flake away, falling down around them and disappearing. Within only a few minutes, her parents were back to normal and, as far as she could tell, no worse for the ordeal they had been through.

Upstairs, she used more vials to release Liore and Tilson from their petrification. Tilson, apparently unaware of the passage of time between when he had been turned to stone and where he was at now, shrieked at the top of his voice and ran with all his might directly into the wall two feet in front of him. He crumpled into a ball on the shelf, cradling his head and whimpering in fear.

"You're okay," Morgan reassured him as she picked him up to hold him close. "I've got you and you're safe. Everything is going to be all right now."

Morgan's adventures as the Chosen will
conclude in

Offering of Surrender
Chronicles of the Chosen, book 5

Available October, 2026

Keep reading for an exclusive sneak peek!

Pebbles fell to the floor, sending echoes of sound bouncing down the dark tunnels. The ground was uneven, with rough boulders embedded in every surface, requiring all who traveled down the pathway to twist and contort into strange shapes in order to pass through. Flickering torchlight created strange shadowy formations to move around, jumping from wall to ceiling to floor as though they were guarding the area against intrusions. As the small group squeezed through tight openings, they knocked portions of the tunnel down, sending more pebbles to scatter across the ground.

"Watch where you're going," the leader called to the rest of the group. "Dropping the whole cavern system down on us is not in the plans for today."

"Yes, Meister," the man in the lead replied. "I will try to be more careful."

They continued down the tunnel, the same tunnels they had already been following for the better part of two days. Sunlight was quickly becoming a distant memory as the oppressive gloom held them captive. Finally the narrow, dangerous red-brown tunnels leveled out onto large panels of open smooth grey stone floor, with fissures running between each of the panels like cracks in the foundation of a building. Each panel was lined with ancient carvings, weathered away so that most were indecipherable. The cracks between panels were different sizes, some narrow enough to barely fit a piece of paper through and others wide enough that required the group of explorers to take turns leaping the chasm. At one of the cracks, a slight wind blew up from beneath the ground, cold cavern air mixing with warm breeze.

The squares continued even as the cavern opened into a massive area, where water flowed far beneath the ground, visible in the cracks between flooring squares. Dim light shone throughout the cavern, small orbs of glowing light slowly drifting in the air, lighting up the area enough that the torches were no longer necessary. Only a short distance into the cavern, a section of the pathway was missing entirely, nothing but a gaping yaw of open air to support their continued journey. That same light glinted off the water far below, flickering reflections adding more light to an already surreal scene.

"What are those glowing things?"

"Will-o-wisps. They're harmless. Keep moving."

"But we cannot, Meister, there is no floor to move upon."

The man called Meister waved his arm and the entire group rose into the air, levitating in place. "I said move."

Without further argument or disagreement, the group continued, walking across empty air.

The floor beneath their feet became less steady as they moved, pieces of ancient stone crumbling away. The further they traveled into the room, the more precarious their position proved to be, as the platform upon which they walked rose in elevation, held aloft by nothing more than a series of ancient pillars, carvings long since lost to the ages. Around them, more walkways supported by more pillars joined their own, some still intact but most long since having fallen into the water below. Taller and taller pillars appeared, most with remnants of the ancient walkway still visible atop but most simply ending in broken points. Stone stairways led from one level to another, some attached at both ends and others leading to nothing at all.

All of the walkways appeared to converge on a central point, a platform that was much larger and seemed to be more stable than any of the others. It was on this platform that the Meister finally gave the signal to stop. "This is it. Begin setting up the supplies."

More torches, with small canisters of fuel suspended on tall poles, surrounded the platform, their light quickly surpassing the dim, eerie glow of the will-o-wisps. Once all of the torches were placed and lit, the leader of the small group stepped to the center of the platform. There, he settled into a cross-legged seated position in the area his men had cleared out for him, closing his eyes and focusing his energy. Runes embedded in his skin began to glow as more of his power activated.

His men stood around him in guard positions, watching out to ensure that nothing interrupted their Meister's work.

After life growing up in the beautifully rainy Pacific Northwest, Shanon L. Mayer tends to keep indoors, writing story after story, building vivid worlds on paper while her thoughts hold everything but images. She tends to look at everything in her world for inspiration – especially her collections of skulls, dragon statues, swords and knives, and pretty much anything that fits her eclectic, geeky-gothic lifestyle.

When her busy life feels like too much, she can be found relaxing with a hot mug of tea and a documentary on anything from theoretical physics to deep ocean wildlife to the most famous heists the world has ever seen.